"KIM'S UNPLANNED SAGA"

IT STARTS WITH A DEATH PENALTY CRIME COMMITTED. KIM IS PUNISHED FOR BEING THE SHERIFF'S DAUGHTER, AND ENDS UP DOING THE UNTHINKABLE. PHYLLIS A. COLLMANN'S STORY TAKES MANY TURNS AND ENDS UP GOING OUT OF THE COUNTRY TO CATCH A KILLER. THE KILLER IS VICIOUS AND CUNNING AND TAKES ADVANTAGE OF THE POOR.

PHYLLIS A. COLLMANN

AUTHOR OF

ROSE'S BETRAYAL AND SURVIVAL
AND
KIM'S UNPLANNED SAGA

DEDICATED TO
MY HUSBAND OF SIXTY YEARS
COLIN R. C. COLLMANN
AND MY CHILDREN
CYNTHIA, KIMBERLY, RONALD
AND MELONIE
I LOVE YOU ALL

ABOUT THE AUTHOR

PHYLLIS A. COLLMANN IS A RETIRED NURSE WHOSE INTEREST IN ADVENTUROUS STORIES LED HER TO WRITE HER OWN.

PHYLLIS LIVES WITH HER HUSBAND OF SIXTY YEARS. SHE LOVES MUSIC, POETRY, AND THE FINE ARTS.

THIS IS PHYLLIS A. COLLMANN'S SECOND BOOK OF NATURE, STRUGGLES, AND HUMAN TRIALS.

ALSO BY PHYLLIS A. COLLMANN
ROSE'S BETRAYAL AND SURVIVAL
AND
KIM'S UNPLANNED SAGA

A SPECIAL THANKS TO
VIKKI EILTS
DIANE TEN NAPEL
AND
REV. ROBERT L. GRUPP

KIM'S UNPLANNED SAGA

Kim had worked late. She walked across the dark parking lot to her car. The girls in her office had been complaining about the parking lot being so scary after dark. They had asked the company to provide more light. She understood now, it was frightening.

She opened her car door, got in with her brief case. Kim knew exactly what it was when she reached into the back seat to lay her briefcase on the seat. Someone's leg.

Someone had broken into her car. Her heart quickened its beat and she thought she could hear it pounding. Her breath came in little fast puffs. Suddenly she was cold.

Kim didn't or couldn't say anything.

The voice from the back seat was low and definitely male. He said, "Drive lady, and do not speed, stay right on this highway till I tell you to turn.

Kim tried to analyze the situation. He had broken into her car, he didn't want her to speed. Her first thought was, he is a criminal. He didn't want her to get stopped by the police. What was he going to do to her and with her?

Kim had a phone, but it was in her purse. Her mother called her frequently. Why didn't she call her now? He would know if she tried to open her purse, any sudden move, and she didn't know what he would do.

Kim looked quickly into the mirror to see -if she could get a glimpse of him. He didn't want her to see him, so he was sitting far enough over so he could not be seen.

She thought she would get him to talk to her. Kim said, "I'm going to need gas soon."

"Drive, just drive," he yelled back at her.

Kim tried again, "Please, the gas stations will all close soon."

"All right, all right, stop at the next station, I'm going to warn you only once, if you try to contact someone, I'm going to kill you lady!"

Kim knew by the sound of his voice he meant what he was saying.

When Kim saw the gas station ahead she slowed the car and pulled in. He quickly reached up to the front seat and took her purse. He took money out of her billfold and handed it to her. Her mind was racing, she could step out of the car and run, but would he shoot her when she was running? When she went into the station, she could tell the serviceman, but if he saw her talking, he would kill her for sure.

While putting gas in her car, she would try to get a glimpse of him. She stepped out of the car, and while filling it with gas, he leaned back so she could not see him at all. Kim walked swiftly into the station, handed the money to the cashier and returned to her car.

She feared he would shoot her and the innocent cashier. At this point Kim thought she could only do what he wanted.

"Now turn the car around," he said, "We're going back to your house."

"No, Kim said, "Just let me go, you can have the car."

"I need you, the car, and supplies. We're heading for the mountains." He told her.

She kept saying to herself, "This is a bad dream and I'll wake up any minute." But a small little voice inside of her said, Kim, you have to outwit him.

Kim drove to her house and parked the car in the garage. He got out of the car after Kim did and walked behind her. She slipped the key into the lock, unlocked the door and they both stepped in. Kim turned to shut the door, and the face she saw was not the face of a criminal. She thought he looked scared and afraid. In fact, she thought he looked more scared than she was, and he looked so young.

But he was still in charge. He ordered her to pack all of the food she had, warm clothing, blankets, and bring all of the money she had in the house.

He questioned her, why she did not have more food in her house.

Kim refused to answer. It took only a few minutes, because he was pushing her to hurry. In a total of fifteen minutes they were ready. Then he told her to sit down on a chair.

Tying her securely to the chair, he said, "I need some rest before we leave."

Kim could not sleep, and she could hear his heavy breathing coming from her bedroom. She also could not move, the end of the rope was in his hand and any movement on her part he could feel immediately. He had been very clever so far.

It was daylight when he awoke. He took the rope off of Kim, and then told her to call her office and tell them she was sick and would not be in for several days.

"Where are you taking me?" Kim asked, "I need to know." Her voice sounded angry.

"You don't need to know anything, and I'm not telling you." he said.

Kim called her office and left a message. Then he said, "Call your family and tell them you have to go out of town for a week because of your job. Tell them you will call as soon as you get back."

CHAPTER 2

He was on his feet wanting to get started. He only wanted to make one trip to the car, so between them they carried it all.

Kim started the car and slowly pulled out onto the street. He pointed to the direction that she should go. Kim knew her life could end at any time, so she did not want to upset him and have him carry out his threats on her.

She realized if he had wanted to rape her, he would have done it already, in her own home.

He sat in the front seat beside her and said, "Just so you understand, I'm not afraid to use this," as he pulled his jacket back to reveal his gun.

The long drive started and the city soon faded behind them. He was directing her to the mountains, and the road was becoming winding, narrow, and steep. After many hours of driving Kim asked him if they could stop. She needed to go to the bathroom. They drove a few more miles before they found a level area to stop.

He told her to wait. He got out, reached into the back seat for a rope, and proceeded to tie it around Kim's waist. She could only go so far into the brush. Kim thought again how clever he was, he had thought of everything.

Kim could not get the thought out of her mind, how did he find her? The parking lot was full of cars, why her? What was he going to do to her, and with her, when they arrived at their destination? Kim was not only scared, but she was totally agitated.

Her thinking was being blocked now, but when she calmed down she would think everything through more clearing.

Kim's father was the sheriff of the county. He was strong and firm, and ran his office strict, but fair. Then Kim started thinking of other ideas. Maybe the kidnapper was looking for her for reasons only he knew, but she was unable to figure it out at this time.

Kim tried to talk to the stranger, so she asked him, "What is your name?" She asked him several times. He told her, "Keep quiet and just drive." He told her what roads to turn off and then on to. A couple of times he told Kim to turn, and she realized he was making her backtrack. She guessed it was to make sure they were not being followed.

The road was getting more narrow and steeper. Kim mentioned to him they had used a lot of gas, and she also complained about how hungry she was.

Finally, he answered her, "We're almost there." After nearly another hour of driving, the brush was getting thicker, the trees tall and close together, the road had turned into a trail.

It was nearly dark. They had driven most of the day, winding their way up the mountain. Kim's thoughts almost made her panic. No one would ever find her. The area was mangled with overgrown vines, weeds and trees. He finally told her, "Park the car."

The young man reached over and put handcuffs around her wrist, and the other around the steering wheel. He said, "I have a lot of work to do and I don't want you running off."

He started by carrying limbs back over the trail, and when he had finished, you could not even tell there was a road or trail there. After he had completely hidden the trail and the car, he unlocked Kim's handcuffs. She wondered how long they would travel by foot, because there wasn't a building in sight.

They carried all they could, it was horrible for her. The vines and underbrush scratched her face and hands. He pushed her in front of him, and at times Kim had to shut her eyes to get through the underbrush.

Kim was cold, and the air was thin and made her short of breath. She knew her family would not start looking for her for a week. What was it he wanted with her?

After walking for some time, Kim could make out something up ahead. The gray, weather-beaten building must have been a haven for hunters a long time ago. It looked like it had not been used for years.

CHAPTER 3

As they approached the cabin Kim saw the large bear hide hanging stretched out on the wall near the door.

The young man opened the door with his key. He had to have been there recently to have his own key, and the padlock looked new. He stepped back and shoved Kim inside. Kim thought it isn't much, but by this time she was cold, tired, and it meant being warm again. She dropped her belongings on the floor. She told him how cold she was, and how dark it was in there.

The stove had wood in it. He had been here before, because he was all prepared. He lit the fire. As he did, she nearly jumped out of her skin. The cabin walls were covered with animal hides. Heads of every animal the mountain made a home for, hung on the wall.

He grabbed her arm, and handcuffed her to a table leg.

He had to go back to the car. They needed everything, including all of the food supplies. He emptied the car of all the supplies.

Kim realized the only way anyone would ever find her would have to be by air. And why would anyone even look on top of this mountain for her?

One of the first things Kim noticed was a radio. It was battery operated, new batteries laid next to it. She felt she had a small connection to the outside world.

Kim offered to help get something to eat. He was reluctant to take the cuffs off of her, so she tried to get him to talk to her.

Kim began by saying, "Do you know my father?"

He answered by saying, "who doesn't know your father?'

Kim began to put the pieces together. She didn't say anything. She was busy trying to think of something to say that would keep him talking.

She said, "He's really a wonderful man, so good and fair, he never cheats a prisoner out of his rights."

The young man was instantly furious. Kim then knew she was his prisoner because of something her father had done in his capacity of sheriff. Ok Kim thought, now I understand, he was waiting and looking, just for me.

She tried to continue talking to him, but he told her to "Shut up or I'll tape your mouth shut." Kim could tell by the supper they ate that food was going to be rationed. They had gone all day without eating, and she was still hungry when they had finished their meal.

Kim had seen young men angry, her own brother could lose his temper if pushed too far, but this young man was on the edge of destruction. He was carrying a very big burden on his mind.

The rooms were small, so it didn't take long before it warmed up, making them both sleepy. He insisted Kim get ready for bed. He hung a blanket on a wire between the two beds, so she had a small amount of privacy. When Kim was ready for bed, he put a handcuff on her wrist, and the other on the bedpost.

Within seconds Kim could hear his heavy breathing. Sleep didn't come easy for Kim, because all of her thoughts and the night noises were keeping her awake. It sounded as if the animal noises were just outside of the door. Then she heard a high-pitched cry, and she knew it was a large cat of some kind. She was not used to hearing strange animal noises. She was used to car noises and delivery trucks. Kim finally pulled her covers over her head to blot out all of the unusual sounds.

Kim thought about his roughness, but she couldn't visualize him truly being like this. Something about the way he moved, and the way he talked when he was not angry. She decided she would show him only kindness, and when the time was right, she would try to escape.

The following morning she was sitting on the edge of her bed. She sat looking at him. He looked so peaceful. He didn't look mean.

"Why was he doing this?" she said to herself.

He woke and quickly checked her handcuffs.

Kim greeted him warmly, saying, "I hope you rested well." He looked at her, not trusting her at all. Kim asked if she could go to the bathroom. He moved toward her to unlock her from the bed, then led her to the bathroom.

Kim politely said, "Thank you." The look he gave her was one of disbelief, as he locked the bathroom door from the outside.

The bathroom had no windows. The water in the cabin was pumped by a generator from water running out of the mountain. The toilet was flushed into a septic tank with the solids being destroyed with acid. The water to bathe in came out of a pipe. There was no faucet. The water ran into a large basin and was extremely cold. The only way to bathe in warm water was to first heat it on the stove, and then carry it into the bathroom. Kim's only worry was to get away, not taking a bath.

When she knocked on the door, he opened it, came in and put the handcuffs back on her. Kim made a point of getting her body close to him. He had not touched her up to now, so she thought she would wear him down. If he had been going to attack her, he would have done it by now.

Kim was planning her escape very carefully. She had to get him to trust her so he would take the handcuffs off, and leave them off He led her to a chair and handcuffed her to it.

"Please tell me your name," she asked. He didn't answer.

He made breakfast and they sat eating in silence.

"My name is Philip, Philip Morrison."

"Philip Morrison," Kim repeated it slowly. She tried to remember if she had heard or read anything about that name. "I don't think I know you," Kim said.

"If you ask your father, he would know the name," Philip answered with rage in his voice.

"I'm sorry Philip, I really don't recognize your name."

He abruptly stood up, walked to the door, went outside and carried in wood. He brought in enough for the night hours and enough for the next day.

He refused to talk to her for the rest of the morning until Kim finally asked if he would let her go outside, just to get some fresh air. It was beginning to snow. She could tell that he really didn't want to.

He uncuffed her from the chair and put the other cuff on his wrist. Kim was not going anywhere without him. Outside, standing on the porch, they noticed the snow was coming down faster and the wind was beginning to blow it around more.

Kim knew any tracks from the car coming up here would surely be gone. Kim moved closer to him, her arm touching his, but he moved away from her. She moved toward him again, her arm pressing on his.

Philip turned his head to look at her. She pretended she was looking at something else, but she knew he was studying her.

She noticed he was wearing a beautiful ring, which had a ruby in the center, with large diamonds all around it. Kim commented on his beautiful ring.

"It was a gift from my parents. When I graduated from Harvard, my aunt bought it for them.

This was more than Kim could comprehend, so she repeated what he had just told her. Philip looked the other way, realizing he had told her more than he planned to. Kim just couldn't let it drop. She wanted him to tell her everything about his life. Philip was agitated, more so at himself, because he had not planned on telling her anything.

"Why would you kidnap me, knowing it's a terrible crime? You're throwing your life away."

He refused to answer, so she knew this was the time to keep quiet.

The snowstorm was turning into an all-out blizzard, and the wind was blowing snow right on them. Philip took her back into the cabin. Upon entering, the room felt cool. Kim mentioned it was cold, so Philip led her over to the stove. She handed him a piece of wood. The thought crossed her mind of hitting him over the head with it, but if something happened to him, Kim thought she probably would not survive.

He took her to the table and cuffed her to the table leg while he fixed them something to eat.

Philip turned on the battery-operated radio. This was day two, but nothing was said about the sheriff's daughter being missing.

The wind was howling and they could see more snow coming down. They now had a full-blown blizzard. They both sat looking out of the only window they had. It was getting very cold outside and the cabin had cold air coming in all over.

Now Kim understood why the hunters had papered the walls with animal hides. She thought if they had not, she and Philip would surely freeze in a storm like the one they were in now.

Philip filled the stove again, took the cuffs off of Kim and let her go into the bathroom. He shut the door.

Kim tried to be as quiet as she could. She opened the door very slowly and took a step out, thinking maybe she could surprise Philip and cuff him to the bed. She knew she would have to hit him with something, and the only thing in the bathroom was a plastic pail. Kim had the pail in her hand as she took another step away from the bathroom.

Philip was standing right beside her, he had been standing next to the door. His hand reached out and "What were you going to do, pail me to death?" He spat at her as he pulled her over to his bed and handcuffed her to it.

Kim wanted to fight him, but she was afraid it would only make him angry. Philip said, "The only reason you're sleeping in my bed is so you won't freeze to death, nothing else. Kim was relieved, but strangely felt a little insulted.

Philip was up every hour keeping the fire going. It was early in the morning when he crawled back into bed after filling the stove again. Kim opened her eyes and caught him staring at her. Her first reaction was to lash out at him, but decided against it.

Her arm was feeling numb. She told him, "I'm in pain from not being able to move my arm." He rolled over the top of her and the blankets and uncuffed her from the bed. He then cuffed her to him.

Kim was so irritated. She raised her free hand and struck out at him. She wished it would have hurt him, but of course, she knew it didn't. He just turned over to go to sleep, and as he turned, he pulled her arm with him. Kim was furious, mortified to think she had to lie next to her captor and be forced to have her arm around him.

She wanted to cry, but at this time, she was just too angry. Later, in the early morning hours Kim calmed down enough to go to sleep.

The blizzard had not let up outside. Kim thought the cabin would be completely covered with snow, and no one would be able to see it from the air. She lay next to him and wondered why she was not as scared as she had been when she discovered Philip in her car. Kim figured she had gone from being scared to being angry, like she felt now.

Philip had interrupted her life. She had gone from a lifestyle of pleasure, having a good paying job, doing the things she liked, to becoming a kidnapped prisoner. Kim was sure the storm would make escaping impossible.

While waiting for the storm to subside, Kim tried to get Philip to talk to her.

"Do you think your family will be looking for you?" she asked.

Suddenly the whole story came tumbling out of Philip.

"Why would they? My only brother is in jail." Philip told her.

"Oh, I'm so sorry, what did he do?", Kim asked sympathetically.

"He didn't do anything wrong, he was at the wrong place at the wrong time." Philip's voice sounded bitter.

"Because your father is the hard-ass keeping him in jail." Philip spat at her. "So now he's going to know what it feels like to have a member of his family taken away from him."

"Oh Philip, this is not right. Now you're going to be in so much trouble. This man you're committing a crime against will search every inch of the earth for me. When he catches you, you will spend the rest of your remaining life behind bars."

Kim began to beg him, "Please Philip, take me back before they know I'm missing. We could get down the mountain in a day or two, I'll never mention your name."

He sat across the table from her with their arms hooked together with the handcuffs.

"What about my brother? What do I do about him?" Philip asked with agitation in his voice.

"Philip, if your brother did not do anything to be jailed for, I'll help you. I'll see to it you get the best lawyer money can pay for. I'll talk to my father, I promise you," Kim continued to plead.

After Kim told Philip of the trouble he would be in, and the charge of kidnapping that would be brought against him, Philip slowly lowered his head. He laid his head down on his arm with the handcuff on it. Kim sat looking at the top of his head. His soft black hair was touching her hand. When this journey started, Kim thought she hated him, now she was beginning to wonder how she felt.

Philip wanted to believe her, but now everything had changed. He had kidnapped the sheriff's daughter. What would happen to him if Kim told her father the truth?

Philip turned the radio on. This was day three, and the news was about the weather.

He hoped his young brother was OK. Philip had been so busy at college, trying to get an education, so he could take care of his brother Will.

His brother Will had gone to live with their mother's sister, after their parents had been killed in a car accident.

Will started running around with some rough kids. Their aunt had called Philip several times asking for advice. Will was staying out past curfew, and was failing in school. His best friend was always with him, but the boys they chose to run with were much older.

Philip told his aunt, "I have two months of college left, before graduation. After graduation, I'll come home and get an apartment, Will can live with me and I'll take care of him."

Will was not a bad boy, he wasn't mean and he didn't get into fights. What he didn't realize was the boys he had chosen to run with, were using and selling drugs.

CHAPTER 6

One week before Philip was to graduate, the boys all went out. They met up with a man Will and his best friend had never seen.

Will stood listening to the guys talking, then an argument broke out. The other boys started swinging at the man. One boy hit him so hard he knocked him to the ground. Will could not believe what he saw them do.

This was an old man, and they were beating him up. He didn't have a chance.

Will and his friend did not know what to do. If they tried to help the man, they knew the other boys would turn on them.

They both told each other later, each one had thought of running. If only they had. The beating they would have gotten from the boys would not be as bad as the trouble they were into now.

The man was kicked into unconsciousness. The boys all ran, leaving the man lying in a dark parking lot, bleeding profusely. He had cuts on his face and head, and his body was bruised all over and swollen twice its size. His clothing was nearly torn off.

Will and his friend ran straight for their homes, and Will went directly to his room and dialed 911. He gave only the information where the man could be found, and then hung up.

It didn't take the police long to locate the caller, and Will was arrested and taken into custody. The first and only call Will made was to Philip.

Philip asked his professors to take his final exam early. When Philip left college, he went directly to the police station. The sheriff brought Will from his jail cell to a room so Philip could talk to him. Will began to cry when he saw Philip. The boys stood with their arms around each other crying like they had done when their parents died.

Will told Philip his entire story of what happened. "I didn't do any of it, I didn't lay a hand on him, please, please believe me," Will pleaded. Philip believed what Will was telling him, because Will would never hurt anyone.

When Will's time was up for his visitation, he was taken back to his cell. Philip then went to see the sheriff. The sheriff's s story was altogether different. He believed Will and his friend were in on it *

"You can't prove a thing against Will," Philip kept telling him.

"It's aggravated assault now. If the man dies, it's first degree murder," the sheriff spat at him.

Philip was at the point of shock, as he tried to reason with the sheriff. He told him about their parent's terrible accident. "Will was just a little boy, and I tried to be mother and father to him till I left for college. After I left, Will moved in with our aunt and uncle." Philip continued, he told him, "How much he missed Will when he had to leave him." He told the sheriff, "I love my brother very much."

"What you need to do young man, is get yourself a good lawyer, because the way it looks, you're going to need one badly," the sheriff barked at Philip.

Philip could tell he had gotten nowhere talking to him.

The only lawyer in town was not a lawyer for this kind of case. Philip had a small amount of money, but certainly not enough to hire a good criminal lawyer.

The following week a hearing was held. The boys could all be released on bond. Philip sold almost everything he owned to get the bond money.

The boys were all out on bond while the man was lying unconscious in the hospital. His brain swollen twice its size, but the best part, he was still alive.

Philip and Will stayed in their aunt's basement talking for hours. Will never changed his story. Philip never let Will out of his sight. When Will's friend called, Philip always told him, "Will is busy."

Philip explained to Will exactly what would happen to all of the boys involved if the man died. He also told Will what the sheriff had told him if the man lived. They had almost killed him, so they were all going to serve some time in prison.

If the man lived, perhaps he could remember all about the argument and the fight. Maybe he could tell the sheriff that Will and his friend did not hit him.

Philip decided he and Will needed to go to the hospital. If they showed their concern to the family it would help them by showing the man's family they cared. Will begged Philip not to make him go.

Philip had taken on a personality of a protector, and insisted Will was going with him. Philip and Will arrived at the hospital while the man's family were all there.

Philip walked down the hall in front of Will. He stopped at the desk and asked about the man's condition and room number. Thank goodness the man was still alive. The swelling on his brain had gone down a small amount, but he had not yet regained consciousness. His family was all in his room, and Philip and Will were not allowed in to see him.

Philip took Will to the waiting room. They sat waiting for a family member. The man's wife came in looking weary and distressed. Philip stood up and introduced himself and Will Morrison. The woman looked intently at Will for a long time. She recognized him. The silence in the room was deafening.

Will moved over behind Philip. Philip was not going to let Will do this. Philip turned and said, "Will, tell the lady what happened."

"I, I, I did not hurt your husband, I never touched him. My friend and I were there, but we did not hurt him." Will stammered.

"If you were there, why didn't you help him?" She asked

"We were scared they would do the same thing to us." Will told her.

Philip told the woman, "It was Will who called for help, please believe him."

The tiny little woman walked slowly up to Will. She took his hands in hers and stood looking into his eyes. Will began to cry. His body was so racked with shame and regret for what he had not done. The woman put her arms around him and held him close.

CHAPTER 7

Philip told Kim, "I felt like that moment was a moment of truth. It wiped away Will's feeling of guilt."

Kim said, "Philip, what happened for you to take the action you did?"

Philip sounded angry telling Kim the story. "Two of the boys broke their bond. They left town and were picked up hiding in an old barn on a farm. The barn was located near the railroad tracks and they were waiting for a train. The owner of the farm spotted them, and called the sheriff."

"The knock on the door was loud," Philip said. And when he opened his aunt's door, Will was arrested again by the sheriff. He handcuffed Will, in front of his family, and took him back to jail."

Will would wait in jail till the man either awoke from unconsciousness, or died from the beating.

Philip said, "I decided all the things the sheriff did to Will, I would do to a member of the sheriff's family."

Philip finally told Kim, why it was her he had taken. "I spent my time investigating your family. I would have coffee in the morning at the town's only cafe and talk to anyone who would talk to me. Casually, I would mention the sheriff. What a good guy he was, and what a good job he was doing. I could get most everyone to talk to me and tell me something I wanted to hear."

"That's when I learned about you, Kim." He was confessing everything. "I started to follow you, I was sure you did not see me, I was feeling smug."

Philip went on to say, "The night I broke into your car, I really tried to act tough."

Kim replied, "I thought you were really going to kill me if I didn't do what you said, Philip. What would you have done if I had not done as you said?"

"I don't know Kim, I don't know." Philip answered.

Philip turned the radio on, this was day three, and nothing was said about Kim being missing. They went through the day in the usual manner. Their meals were eaten, and at each meal, Kim looked at him wondering what it would have been like if she had met him under different circumstances.

The following morning was day four. Philip continued to cuff her. He could not let anything happen to her, and he could not let her get away. By mid-morning he complained of not feeling well. He was really ill, and he had to vomit.

Kim insisted he take the cuffs off of her, in case he needed her help. Philip handed Kim the key, and went into the bathroom and closed the door. Kim could hear him being sick.

Kim was out of the door carrying her coat. She was heading down the mountain. The snow was so deep that her feet sunk down into the snow up to her knees. It only took a short time and she was out of breath. Her legs were beginning to ache, because she had been locked up for four days, and had no exercise. Every step was painful.

The tumble she took was fast, her feet went first and she could not stop at all. She was falling deep into a small area.

When she stopped sliding down, her feet struck something and she was standing upright in a ravine. It was so narrow Kim could not move, she couldn't even turn. Her lungs hurt when she took a breath, because she was breathing in snow through her nose and mouth.

It took only a few minutes, for her to realize she could die here and now.

Philip opened the door of the bathroom and looked for Kim. Kim was gone. Now Kim was forcing him to go out in the freezing weather to look for her. He knew he would die in the electric chair if anything happened to her.

He lost her tracks a couple of times, because the wind was blowing snow over them. He looked in every direction while calling her name, then he would stop and listen. The sound was so faint. He hurried toward it.

Philip looked down the opening, he could only see the top of her head. He knew there was no way of getting her out without a rope. He lay down on the snow next to the opening and yelled to her.

"Kim, I'm going back to the cabin to get a rope. Stay awake Kim. Stay awake."

He knew he had to hurry or she would freeze. Philip tried to run, but his legs were hurting so badly. He kept picturing Kim frozen when he returned. He pushed himself all the way.

The rope was right where he had left it. He had used it on Kim on the way up the mountain. He knew it took him at least twenty minutes to get back to her,

He lay down next to the narrow opening. He could hear her saying, "I'm so cold, I'm so cold."

"Kim, Kim, listen to me." Philip called to her.

"Kim, I'm throwing you the rope, grab the end, and hang on to it and I'll pull you up." Philip commanded. Kim tried, she grabbed the rope, but it slipped right out of her hands. Her hands were too cold to hang onto it.

Philip pulled the rope back up, and explained to her that he was making a slipknot on the end of the rope. He made the loop big enough for her to slip over her head and put her arms through.

"Kim, answer me please." He begged.

"Philip, this is all your fault." She spat at him.

It took another fifteen minutes to get the rope in place. Each time she moved she felt as though she was dropping farther into the ravine. She knew if she didn't get the rope under her arms she would die right there.

Kim's voice was sounding like a moan now. Philip began pulling her slowly up. She was covered with snow, and the process was painful for her. He pulled her completely out and she laid face down in the snow.

Philip quickly turned her over and cleaned the snow off of her face so she could get her breath. The sound she made was a moan.

He picked her up, lifted her up over his shoulder. He struggled through the snow. Kim moaned all of the way.

The pain in his legs was almost unbearable, his shoulder felt numb, his back felt like it would break any minute. He staggered into the cabin, reached back and slammed the door.

Philip leaned over the bed and dropped her. Kim was like a large mannequin of ice, she couldn't even bend.

Philip filled the stove with wood. Then tore off her coat, covered her frozen body. He knew she would die if he didn't do something else.

Kim was making a high-pitched squeak. Her hair was full of snow and was stiff. He wondered how she could breath; her nose was full of frozen snow. He cleared her nose and ears.

Philip put a pan of water on top of the stove to get hot.

Next, he removed all of Kim's frozen clothes. Then Philip took all of his clothes off. He crawled into bed, and on top of her. He rubbed her sides with both of his hands. His body covered her completely. He held her close and breathed his warm breath on her face and neck.

He refilled the stove every hour. When the water was hot, he forced her to drink at least one cup each hour. He was trying to warm her in the inside too.

By morning Kim was squirming from Philip's weight on her. All of a sudden Kim realized Philip's naked body was laying on her. She felt every part of his body on her.

She tried to push him off. She wanted to fight him, but her body was too weak. She began screaming at him.

He grabbed her arm and cuffed it to her bed. Philip would never trust her again. He would protect her at any cost, because she was dangerous to herself and him.

He dressed in the bathroom, while she continued to scream at him.

CHAPTER 8

Kim lay in bed wondering what happened during the night. Did they or didn't they? She remembered how cold she was. The feeling she had knowing she was freezing to death. When she calmed down and was rational, she knew Philip had saved her life, but even then it was still his entire fault.

Philip told her, "Wrap a blanket around you and go get dressed." He had removed everything out of the bathroom that she could possibly hit him with.

He was standing next to the door when she opened it. Again she was handcuffed and set at the table with the other cuff on the table leg.

While Philip was getting their breakfast, they listened to the radio. This was day five. He was hoping to hear some news on the unconscious man. Philip was at the radio turning up the volume. The announcer continued, there was no change in the man's condition. The family was at his bedside in an all-night vigil. The young men accused of this terrible beating remained in the county jail, and would remain there until the man's condition changed

The news announcer had said nothing about Kim. No one was aware she was missing.

"Your father will know in two days how it feels to miss someone he loves. All I've ever wanted was to take care of Will, and protect him. Your father can not protect you now." Philip growled.

Kim raised her voice, "Philip, when my father finds you, he will shoot you first and then ask questions."

"He'll have to find us first, won't he Kim?" Philip was becoming agitated. "We'll hunt, fish and pick berries. We can live up here for a very long time." Philip told her.

A shiver went up Kim's back she knew he meant every word he was saying.

Kim never wasted a chance to learn more about him. He told her he grew up in a very loving family. His parents were well educated, and they both taught school. It was a school meeting they were coming home from when the car accident happened.

A large trust fund was in their names, but they had to be twenty-five to be able to use it. It was now Philip needed the money. A criminal lawyer was very expensive.

At times Kim wanted to put her arms around him and tell him it would be all right. She didn't want to feel this way. She kept telling herself she could die upon this mountain, and her family would never know her whereabouts. This was all his fault.

Philip wished he had brought more food. It was taking more than he had planned. The mountains were full of deer. Actually it was full of all kinds of animals. The thought of eating any other animal meat, but deer, did not appeal to him.

Her father had taught her how to shoot. After she told him, he acted and sounded mad and offended.

He gave her a choice of where she wanted to be while he went out. Philip checked the cuffs. Kim decided to sit at the table and wait for him.

"I'll be back as soon as I can," he told her as he left the cabin.

By the time Philip returned, Kim was tired of sitting on the chair, tired of not being able to move, tired of feeling sorry for him. As Philip opened the door, she was hollering at him.

"Why were you gone so long? Where is the deer? I need to go to the bathroom. I'm really hungry."

Philip didn't answer. He put the gun back in the case. He walked over to her, removed the handcuffs and took her to the bathroom.

"You didn't get anything did you?" Kim said. She just couldn't let it drop. Philip slammed the bathroom door. She knew he was not going to answer.

He let her walk around in the cabin before he cuffed her to the table again. Philip prepared what little food they had for dinner.

CHAPTER 9

He turned on the radio. This was day six. They sat anxiously waiting to hear if the news had something about the unconscious man. There was no news about him today.

Kim wanted to change the feeling of hopelessness in the cabin. She began by saying, "Maybe I should go hunting with you in the morning, because my father taught me a lot about hunting."

"Your father only knows how to hurt people." Philip retorted at her. Kim decided she would not mention her father's name when she was trying to get Philip to do something.

"Kim, maybe if you would have had more food in your home, we wouldn't have to go out in this freezing weather." Philip's voice sounded sarcastic.

Kim ignored the remark.

"I promise Philip, I won't run away. Please let me help you. I've done this many times before." She tried hard to convince him.

The following morning was day seven. Philip turned the radio on while making breakfast. The first news of the day started with a story about the sheriff's daughter.

The news announcer stated, "If anyone had seen Kim Conrad, call the sheriff's office immediately.

The company Kim worked for called her parent's house, asking if Kim was feeling better. Kim's parents told her boss she had left a message saying she was on a business trip. Suddenly everyone was concerned over Kim's whereabouts, and now they were looking for her.

Philip felt sick, his stomach was rolling. He felt like he would lose his breakfast any minute. He knew he was in more trouble than he could even imagine.

The room was dead silent, except for the sound of their breathing. Kim could hear Philip's breaths. They sounded as if he was gasping for air. His eyes had a sullen glaze over them. Then the voice on the radio changed.

Kim said," Oh my God, it's my father." She listened, mulling over what she was hearing. His voice sounded different, not firm and strong like she was used to. His voice sounded strained, weary and very concerned. Kim ached to be able to tell him she was all right and not to worry, she was sure Philip would never harm her.

Her father was asking, "Anyone who has seen her recently, please call my office." He went on to say, "We have not seen her in a week, and everyone is concerned. Kim, we love you so much, please take care of yourself and please call us if you can. Ben sends his love. He also wants you to know you still owe him $5.00."

Philip got up and turned the radio off. This was the news he had wanted to hear. It didn't feel like he thought it was going to. It didn't feel like pay back. It felt like pain. He went into the bathroom and slammed the door. Within minutes, Kim could hear Philip sobbing, and she knew he felt as bad as she did, as she sat sobbing.

When Philip composed himself, he came out and told Kim, "Even if we wanted to go back we couldn't make it down the mountain because the snow is so deep. I don't think we can even find the car."

"Kim," Philip said, "Is Ben one of your brothers?"

"No Philip, Ben is my only brother, he's my hero." Kim's voice cracked.

"Then you know how I feel." Philip said.

"The difference is, I don't think I'd have resorted to your actions." Kim replied.

"You have a family, I have no one." Philip was not going to give in, not yet.

The rest of the day they didn't talk, there was just too much to think about. The temperature in the cabin was dropping, as it was getting colder outside. Philip got up several times during the night to put wood in the stove. When morning arrived nothing had changed, they still needed food.

The one thing Philip had to do was swallow his pride. He needed Kim's help. He approached her by asking if she would like to help get breakfast.

Kim wanted to yell at him and say, "With my handcuffs on," but decided against it.

"Yes Philip, I want to help." She said instead.

He then asked if she wanted to go hunting with him, and she readily agreed to that. He explained, "It is very treacherous with rocks under the snow. The snow is deep and if we take a wrong step we could slip off of a cliff. Breaking a leg could mean death."

Kim was ready long before Philip. Her gun was cleaned and loaded. She never wanted to be cold again, but the thought of being hungry was urging her to go out in the freezing weather and hunt. The other reasons were, the handcuffs were off and they were getting out of the cabin.

Philip fixed her snowshoes, as they were a large man's size. The snowshoes and skis were always left in the cabin for any hunters coming to the mountain to hunt.

The cold, crisp air hit her face. She pulled her scarf up. Philip explained what they were going to do, "I'll go first, to open up steps for you, and we'll continually circle the cabin, going out further each time."

Finally he said, "Kim, I'm trusting you, because you will be behind me with your loaded gun."

Of course, Kim was not going to mention the thought had already entered her mind.

The tracks they both saw were rabbit. The rabbit was squatted low, trying to hide. Philip decided instantly to let Kim shoot first, because if she missed, he could shoot. If he missed, at least she couldn't harass him. He nodded for her to shoot. She aimed and fired. The rabbit lay motionless on the snow.

Kim talked Philip through the procedure of skinning the rabbit. They sat across from each other at the supper table. Kim had prepared the rabbit just right. They would share the other half for a meal the next day.

The handcuffs were laying on a shelf in the gun case.

Kim started the conversation by asking Philip, "What can we do to help Will, if he has to stand trial?"

Philip told her, "Will's only hope is to convince the jury that he didn't take part in the cruel beating. If the man dies, he will never be able to prove it, and he could spend the rest of his life in prison."

Kim kept pressing him, "We need to get back to help Will." Kim watched as he turned solemn, but he never answered her.

Philip was sure it would be several days before they could even attempt to go back down the mountain. The afternoon passed and they were polite to each other. The cuffs remained off.

Kim said, "I have some money saved, I could help pay for a lawyer for Will." Again she stunned him enough that he couldn't even look at her, so he just looked out the window. Philip wanted to trust her, but this was unbelievable.

Kim found herself looking at him many times, wondering what happened the night he laid on her nude body. Philip denied anything happened.

Philip finally said, "We need to get ready to go hunting in the morning. We need to clean our guns." He wanted to talk about the direction they would go, and what they would do, in case they became separated.

The wind was howling all night and they found it almost impossible to sleep. As soon as it became daylight they turned the radio on to catch the latest news. The announcer was saying, a large reward was being offered by the family, for any information about Kim Conrad. The family was feeling anguish about her safety. They were asking the public to call the sheriff's office if anyone had seen her or knew of her whereabouts.

Kim turned the radio off. She was safe. Philip would never hurt her, she felt sure of that. She was more concerned about what her father would do to Philip.

CHAPTER 10

The wind chill made it feel like 20 below, so every time going out of the cabin was a dangerous risk. Kim tried to talk him out of leaving the cabin.

She said, "Philip, this is a big mistake. Let's just set some traps and try to catch some rabbits, I've seen rabbits from the window and I've heard animals around the cabin at night."

Philip answered by saying, "If we can get to the decoy, we could get a deer, and we would have enough food till the weather clears. Then we can start down the mountain."

He had made up his mind. They were going out to the decoy to hunt. Philip told her several times what would happen if they were separated, or if they got lost.

He told her all about the decoy he had discovered when he came up to prepare for bringing her here. It was a hiding place hunters sat in while waiting for deer, antelope or any other animal coming to this area to eat.

The only difference was, the hunters came in the spring, summer, or fall. Once the first snow fell, you could be snowed in for weeks.

Philip hoped he could find the lookout area. The wind was so strong and the snow stung against their face. They both covered their faces, with only their eyes showing.

Philip found the hideaway. It was covered with snow. He dug out as much as he could so they both could get undercover. They crawled into the small opening and sat down close together. Their guns lay in front of them. They sat huddled together in silence.

Then Philip whispered to her, "Kim, I'm sorry for what I've done, I'm sorry I got you into this mess, you really don't deserve what I've done to you.

"Philip, please do not ask me to forgive you right now, because it's going to take me along time to work through this situation. The one thing I can tell you," Kim said, "I'll never turn against you."

Kim was getting very cold, she moved closer to him. They sat for what seemed like hours, and nothing appeared, "Philip, I'm so cold, please let's go back, we can try tomorrow," Kim begged.

Of course, Philip's ego was beginning to show, because this was the second time he had tried his skill at hunting and had failed Without a word he started to move. He got up, reached his hand back to help Kim up.

The trip back to the cabin was grueling for them both. The wind was blowing the snow so their vision was almost impossible. Their tracks were now all gone. Philip was ahead pulling her and trying so hard to remember the way back to the cabin. He made a wrong turn and now they were lost.

He felt sick and his chest was beginning to hurt. His body was shivering from the freezing cold Kim knew they were lost, and wanted to tell him, "This is all your fault." But she knew he wouldn't be able to hear her anyway.

She fell several times, and her legs were feeling hard and numb. Philip picked her up. He had slung both rifles over his shoulder. He was taking one step at a time. He struggled back to where he thought he had made a wrong turn. He made the turn. And every step was torture for him.

When Philip saw a glimpse of the cabin through the blowing snow, he started to cry. He was sobbing by the time he opened the door. Philip dragged her into the cabin. He stood her near the stove, started the fire and made her keep moving, walking around and around the stove.

They both were in excruciating pain when they began to thaw out. He insisted they keep moving until they were warm.

They had a small amount of food for supper. Philip told Kim, "We will have to ration what food we have left. Also, we are running out of kerosene for the lamp. We can only keep it lit a short time each night.

Kim asked if, "He would help her set traps outside of the cabin?" She thought he acted like he was pouting, so she tried not to be bossy. She explained how they would set the traps while they were in the cabin, so when they went outside it would not take so long. Philip helped without saying a word.

Philip checked the traps early in the morning, as soon as the sun was coming up. When he found the first trap had a rabbit in it, he was so relieved; they could eat two meals off the rabbit. The second trap had a raccoon in it. They would set traps every night.

Philip wanted to turn the radio on, but each time it felt like a knife being stuck into his heart. This was day nine.

Kim walked by the radio several times before she stopped, and her hand slowly went out and turned the radio on.

"Kim Conrad, if you can hear this, call home please." the newsman continued about her family being so distraught. He mentioned how, "The reward is getting larger, because so many people are worried." Kim felt nauseated. Philip turned his back to the radio.

"The weatherman is watching a storm. If it continues on its present course, it would be at the mountain region by morning." He was warning everyone not to travel. He said, "Stay off of all roads."

Philip turned the radio off, looked at Kim and said, "We're really in trouble now. Let's get the traps set. Maybe we'll be lucky and trap some rabbits before the storm gets here.

After the traps were set outside, Philip told her, "I'll listen for the storm to hit and get the traps in before they get covered with snow."

Kim dropped off to sleep and was awakened by the most powerful wind hitting the cabin. She felt as though the cabin would lift off its foundation. The storm was upon them, and now the snow was piling up higher and higher.

Philip had been out many times, bringing in enough wood to last all night and most of the next day. He also brought the three traps in. One trap had a rabbit, one had a raccoon, and the last one had an animal that looked like a large rat. This time he saved all of the animals. He knew how Kim would feel about eating a raccoon, let alone a rat, but she would not have a choice.

He didn't get much sleep. He needed to keep the stove going. The storm continued from midnight till noon the following day. The snow was piled up over the only window they had. The cabin remained warm, because the snow had almost buried it, and so it was well insulated with snow.

Kim took her turn keeping the fire going while Philip went to sleep. She sat on her bed watching him. His sleep was restless and he made moaning noises.

Kim wanted to help him, she wanted to take all of his agonizing pain away. She wondered why she was feeling this way. After all he'd kidnapped her. Now she was feeling sorry for him. And what about her family? How hard this must be for them.

When Philip woke, Kim fixed just enough food for them both to keep from starving.

Philip went to the door to bring in more wood. He could get the door open only a few inches. The snow was up over the door. He stuck his hand out and tried to push some snow away. He worked for over an hour to open the door enough to crawl out. He crawled through the snow to the woodpile, he would crawl back and hand a chunk through the door for Kim to stack inside.

While he was outside, he skinned the rabbit and raccoon, and the animal that looked like a rat.

Without letting Kim see the other animals, they were put in with the rabbit to cook. He picked the meat off of all the animals and mixed them together. Now they had enough meat for a couple more days.

That evening, for supper, he served a small helping of the meat. Kim took a bite, chewed it and swallowed. Philip tried not to look at her. She continued to eat.

"Philip," Kim said, "What are we eating with the rabbit "Just rabbit, Kim." he answered her without looking at her.

"Please, Philip, tell me it's not a rat."

"No, it's not a rat." He stood up and took his plate to the sink to stop the conversation.

That evening passed slowly and they took turns filling the stove.

In the morning they each had a small bowl of cereal, and it seemed each one was waiting for the other to turn the radio on.

CHAPTER 11

Philip turned the radio on and went to the table and sat down directly across from Kim.

"Wong Penn Nai, had awakened from his unconscious state," the announcer stated. "His condition was still critical, but the doctors were hopeful. The boys accused of this crime were still in jail. Kim Conrad was still missing, and a large search was underway. They were searching down every lead they had, and they were going to use airplanes this morning." The announcer ended by saying, "May God have pity on the person or persons, if they have harmed the sheriff's daughter."

Kim jumped to her feet and ran to the radio and turned it off immediately.

She began to sob, she was so mixed up. Why did they have to look for her. She was safe with Philip. He walked to her and took her in his arms, and held her close. And for the first time, she willingly let Philip kiss her.

"Philip," she said, "Will you marry me?"

The surprised shocked look on Philip's face told Kim this was the very last thing he would have expected her to say.

"Kim, I need to think about this," the words tumbled out of Philip's mouth.

"No, Philip, you do not have time to think about it."

"Can you ski?" she asked.

Philip hesitated, then answered, "Of course I can ski."

"Then we need to get off of this mountain, and the only way, is by skis. We can get married as soon as we get there." Kim added

"Why are you willing to do this Kim?" Philip asked.

"Because, Philip," Kim said, "My father will send you to jail forever, or even worse, he'll have you put to death. You are guilty of kidnapping."

It was silent in the cabin the rest of the evening. When they were ready for bed, Kim walked up to Philip and kissed him hard on the mouth.

Then she said, "It won't be so bad having to marry me, will it?" He didn't answer, he just held her close.

When it was nearly light out, Philip thought he heard a plane overhead. He woke Kim, and told her, "We need to make plans about going down the mountain. We can only carry finger food in our backpacks. Kim, we need to dress in layers, so we won't freeze." Kim stood listening intently.

Philip explained how difficult it was going to be. "The first mile, we will have to walk on snow shoes, because of the thick brush and rocks. Kim, you will have to carry your skis. Are you really up to this? If you are not willing to risk your life, we need to stay here. When they send planes out, they will find us."

Kim answered by saying, "Philip, you must understand my father will never quit looking for me. When he finds out what happened to me, you will never be a free man. You will be convicted and put on death row. The only chance you have is to get down the mountain and marry me. We will have to live a lie the rest of our lives."

"Oh Kim, what have I done?" He reached out and took her face in his hands, and repeated it again.

"Philip, do you have a way or route off the mountain?" She was trusting him completely.

He said, "We'll follow the same route down the mountain, as we traveled up here."

"Do you remember it, Philip?" she asked. "The snow will have it all covered."

"You'll just have to depend on me, Kim." Philip replied.

They began preparing. The skis were brought in to polish and fit Kim's boots to the skis. Philip brought in the snowshoes to adjust.

It was decided, if the weather was clear, they would start in the morning. Food was packed in small individual packages, so all they had to do was reach into their backpack and eat. Snow would be used for water.

Before leaving the cabin, Kim turned the radio on one last time. They stood and listened as the announcer said, "Today the sheriff will be making a door to door search asking every individual if they know anything about his daughter." The next news of the day was about Wong Penn Nai, he was showing a little improvement. He could say one or two words now. The young men accused of the beating remained in custody. The newsman went on to talk about the weather being clear and warming.

Philip wanted the fire completely out in the stove before they left the cabin. He stopped putting wood in it. He did not want smoke from the chimney seen by an airplane search.

He decided the clothing they would wear. Philip suggested they wrap their bodies in old newspapers that the hunters had left behind, especially their feet, before putting on their boots. He hoped it would protect them from freezing. He slipped plastic bags over the newspaper they had put over their socks before putting on their boots.

The food was put in their backpacks, if it froze it was all right it had all been cooked.

Philip tried to visualize the trail in his mind. The clouds were so low, they could see only one step at a time. The air made breathing difficult, their breathing was deep and labored.

It was at this time Philip tied a rope around his waist and the other end around Kim's waist. Getting separated could mean death for either one, or both of them.

Philip mentioned he thought they were at the area they left Kim's car, but the car was covered with snow, so it didn't make any difference. Philip hoped he was on the right route down the mountain.

Each step was carefully placed, Philip did not want to hurry, because carrying the skis and poles was most strenuous, and he wanted to conserve their energy. He knew they had to keep from freezing, so he had planned the trip for what he hoped was survival.

CHAPTER 12

Several times Kim fell and Philip felt the rope jerk on his waist. He would stop, drop his skis and go back and pick her up. He put his arms around her and held her. He told her, "Kim please, we have to do this. I know it's all my fault, and I love you for all you've done for Will and me. We have to make sure we are not found."

They started again. Suddenly Philip took a wrong step and went tumbling down an incline. Kim saw him fall and braced herself by dropping down on her bottom and bracing her snowshoes.

Kim was screaming at him to see if he had gotten hurt. "I'm not hurt Kim, I'll be all right in a minute." Philip answered her weakly. He had to untie the rope from around his waist and look for his skis. They had gone flying when he fell. He crawled, searching, till he found his skis and pole, then he found his way back up to Kim. She sat with her head down, looking defeated, and she was extremely cold.

Philip lifted her gently up onto her feet, hugged her tightly and told her, "We'll make it Kim, I promise we'll make it. I think another five hundred feet down and we can use our skis."

It was about midmorning when the clouds lifted. In places rocks were sticking up, making it hard to place their snowshoes, Limbs stuck out and tore at their bodies.

Philip was in front as usual, and Kim pulled on the rope.

Philip stopped and turned back toward her. He had heard the airplane too. He pulled the rope so Kim moved quickly to him.

He dropped to his knees, motioning her to drop down to her knees. They both bent forward so their faces were in the snow.

They stayed motionless in that position until the plane was gone, and they could not hear its engine. "We're OK now," Philip told her.

They again got to their feet, and brushed the snow off. Philip told her, "We'll go till it starts to get dark, and then we'll look for a place we can dig into for shelter till morning."

Because they were moving and using all of their body parts, it kept them from freezing. They carefully placed one foot at a time.

They had gone a couple hundred feet more when Kim noticed a place where the snow hung out over a large boulder.

All Philip could say was, "Perfect."

He got on his knees and began to dig in the snow with his hands. Kim pushed the snow away to make room for more. When he had an opening big enough for both of them to get into and sit, he took a canvas he had in his backpack and spread it out in the small cave and crawled. Kim crawled in and sat next to him. Philip pulled all the edges of the canvas up over them, so their warm body heat would keep them alive till morning, when they could start down the mountain again.

They ate a small amount of food that they had in their backpack and put snow in their mouths for water.

Philip told her several times, "Wake me up if you hear anything unusual, with the airplanes flying overhead, it could cause a snow slide."

Kim was snuggled up next to Philip. It took only a few minutes and they were both sound asleep. Philip awoke first when it got light outside. He moved his body and Kim awoke immediately.

He told her, "We need to get started." She unwrapped herself from the canvas and crawled out. There was a loud noise overhead and the snow was blowing around about them.

Philip grabbed her and pulled her back into the cave. Panic was setting in.

"It's a helicopter Kim, it's right over us, your father is looking for you!" Philip's voice sounded scared

"We'll wait right here Philip, until they are gone." Kim whispered.

They knew the men in the helicopter could not see them from above, that's why they had looked and found the place where they could crawl into from the side.

Philip and Kim sat huddled together, listening for the noise of the helicopter engine to fade away.

Kim's father was on her trail. Did he know something about her whereabouts? Kim wondered how he could have figured out where she was.

Philip interrupted her thoughts, "Kim, we really have to hurry now."

They talked about what they should do if they heard an airplane or another helicopter. The plan was to stop, and dig down into the snow, and cover up as much as they could.

Kim had forgotten how cold she was, her fear of being caught was the only thing she could think of now. Philip thought they only had a few hundred feet to go and then they could put on their skis.

When he stopped and said, "Put on your skis." Kim stood and cried from being so cold and tired. Her arms ached from carrying her skis and pole. He untied the rope from Kim's waist and put his arms around her. She laid her head on his chest.

"Kim, you will have to go first, as I'm sure I do not ski as well as you. All you have to do is pick out the best path you can." Philip told her.

Kim's first thought was how well did Philip ski? She started skiing when she was only three years old. Her father had taken Ben and her out on ski training with his fellow police officers. The mountain area they were in was straight down. Turning and twisting was almost impossible, because of the trees and boulders.

Suddenly, Kim had a bad feeling come over her. She was no longer dependent on Philip. He was putting his trust in her, to get him off of the mountain. He was trusting her to save his life. Kim tried to think of some other way. If she went alone she knew she could make it, but he could get seriously hurt. She didn't want to think of how this all started, because it would only distract her from the most impossible situation she had ever been in. She wanted to keep her mind clear, to think of the trip down the mountain, and not to be seen from the air.

"How much skiing have you done, Philip?" Kim needed to know.

He hesitated and said, I went on a skiing trip when I was a senior in High School." Philip told her. That was not the answer she was hoping to hear.

Kim was getting very cold while they talked and removed their snowshoes. The snowshoes would be tied to their backpacks in case they ran into a problem with skiing. The wind was blowing the snow, and the snow on the limbs was blowing off, making it look like another snowstorm was upon them.

Kim felt she needed to tell him everything she knew about how fast he would be traveling, and how dangerously close he would be to the trees.

She said, "Please, try to keep me in your sight. I'm going to start a couple minutes before you. All you will see of me is a blanket of snow moving. Philip, you must twist and turn your skis to slow down, keep your knees bent. Pull your poles into your body if you're close to trees. Oh Philip, we need to start. Philip, watch, watch me closely." Kim instructed.

Kim's father had been a sheriff all of her life, and his job had taken him onto the mountain to ski many times. He had taken her and her brother along. He had instilled in them the ability and to know the danger of skiing on the mountain.

She found this very difficult, because her body was cold and somewhat stiff. It took her nearly five hundred feet of twisting and turning to feel a small amount of confidence. She tried hard to look ahead and concentrate, because her mind was always behind her, hoping he was coming.

The snow was fluffy and with the wind blowing, Philip could not keep her in sight. He was so busy trying to slow down and keep from hitting the trees, because it was almost straight down.

The first fall he took was when his ski hit a big boulder sticking up that was covered with snow. It sent him tumbling and sliding at least fifty feet. He stopped when his body hit a tree. He lay motionless, he couldn't get his breath. He felt like he was going to pass-out. He started to hyperventilate. His thoughts were all mixed up. Why did he kidnap Kim? Why did he do this to her?

He lay there thinking he was going to freeze within a short time. Then what would happen to Will? His skis were still on, as he struggled to get up, to start again. The last two days were catching up to him. He had not eaten enough, not drank enough liquid, so his strength was ebbing away.

Kim was now, clearly, at least a mile ahead of Philip. She was trying to slow down and find a spot so she could try to see if Philip was coming. It took her at least two hundred feet more before she was able to stop.

Kim cupped her hands around her face, to look back up the mountain, hoping to see a fluff of snow moving toward her.

Kim spotted him. He was coming so fast it scared her. She stood watching the swirling snow puff, and suddenly it stopped. She stood straining her eyes to catch sight of Philip again. Time was slipping by, and no sight of him.

She knew she could not start again without knowing if he was safe. She decided to go back up and look for him. Kim removed her skis, untied her snowshoes from her backpack, picked up her skis and started back toward the swirl of snow she had last seen. The only thing that was keeping her going was her adrenaline. She was extremely exhausted.

Kim tried to find her ski tracks, but the wind continued to blow, and her tracks were disappearing rapidly. She wanted to scream his name out, but her fear of starting an avalanche was on her mind- Kim said his name in a quiet voice over and over.

The steps were very difficult now, because they were straight up. Kim tried to think about something good in her life, and to her amazement all she could think of was Philip. She lost track of time as each step up was making her legs ache.

Kim said his name once again, and then she heard him. Philip was moaning in pain. She could not see him yet, but his moaning was getting louder, so she continued in the direction of the moan.

Philip was laying face down in the snow. One leg was twisted off to the side of his body. Kim gently turned him over while holding his twisted leg. She brushed all the snow off of him. He was in so much pain.

"Philip, oh Philip, your leg is broken." Kim whispered to him.

She unfastened his belt from his jeans, slipped it under his leg. She proceeded to straighten out his leg, then firmly tightened up the belt, while Philip cried out in torturous pain.

"Oh Philip, now we're in a life or death plight." Kim told him sadly.

"Kim, I'm so sorry for what I've done to you, Philip told her one more time.

"We must hurry now, I've got to get you to a hospital as fast as I can." Kim was adamant about it.

She laid her skis next to Philip, crawled around until she had found his skis that had slid away on their own when he fell. When Kim found his skis, she put the four skis together and tied them in a row. Then she made a loop out of the rope Philip had in his backpack, so he could hold on and drive the skis while he was sitting on them.

Kim explained he needed to pull the rope either on the left or right to keep from hitting the trees, as he would be going extremely fast.

Kim tied the end of the rope around the four skis in the back, and held onto the rope to slow him down, while she walked behind on her snowshoes.

CHAPTER 13

It was a horrible ride for Philip, his pain was unbearable at times.

Kim was being pulled so fast, at times she was running. She made a promise to herself that she would not ski again, unless it was an emergency. This, of course, was an emergency.

The noise Kim heard was a motor. It was not an airplane or helicopter. The sound was getting closer and suddenly, it was right beside them. It was the game commissioner, on his snowmobile.

Kim was pulling back on the rope to get the skis to stop. The commissioner reached out and pulled back on the rope to help. She explained to him the story she and Philip had agreed they would tell.

He believed every word. He carefully loaded Philip on his snowmobile, and told them the nearest doctor was a veterinary, a short distant ahead. They should have Philip checked there, then call an ambulance to transport him to the nearest hospital.

Kim rode on the back of the snowmobile. She spent the time practicing what she would tell her father.

The commissioner and the veterinary doctor carried Philip in. Kim's feet and legs were numb and every step was painful.

As the veterinary first cut Philip's pant leg, and removed the plastic bag, and then unwrapped the newspapers, he said, "Philip didn't freeze, because of his insulation." When the veterinary got to his leg, he shook his head and said, "This is a terrible break, we need to get him to the hospital now."

Kim was in the waiting room trying so hard not to cry, because her body was warming and she was hurting all over.

While in the ambulance, Kim leaned over and whispered, "I'm going home, shower, change clothes, and I'll be at the hospital before you have surgery." Kim continued, "Philip, I have to call my mother and father. I have to tell them how you saved my life."

Little tears ran down Philip's cheeks, and Kim tenderly wiped them off.

She walked into the hospital holding Philip's hand. The doctor was waiting to take care of him. She squeezed Philip's hand before she left, to do something she had never done before, and that was lie to her parents.

CHAPTER 14

Her mother's voice sounded sad when she answered the phone. When she heard Kim's voice she screamed, yelled and cried out, "Kim, Kim, where have you been? We have been going out of our minds with worry."

Kim answered with her rehearsed story, "I needed to get away mother, and I drove up into the mountains. The snowstorm came so fast, I couldn't get back. Mother, I need to go to the hospital, the young man that saved my life is having surgery on his broken leg. I'll tell you everything later." Kim hung the phone up before her mother could ask any more questions.

Next she needed to make a quick call to the sheriff. The voice on the other end made her very nervous.

"Daddy, it's Kim, I'm fine. I took a trip up to the mountains with someone I love very much, and the snowstorm moved in so fast, we couldn't get out.

"Kim, Oh Kim, we were so afraid something terrible happened to you. We thought someone crazy had kidnapped you."

"Oh no Daddy, nothing like that." Kim answered him, feeling guilty.

"Kim, I need to make a news broadcast, and let everyone know your safe. Kim, did you call your mother? She nearly went off the deep end," he said.

"Yes Daddy, I called her first." Kim said, while her stomach was churning.

Kim, you need to come with me to the radio station. You need to explain what happened. Does Ben know you're back? Her father was beginning to do what he does very well, question people.

"Daddy, before I do or go anywhere, I need to go to the hospital. My dear friend broke his leg helping me down the mountain, and he is having surgery. Kim's voice was firm.

"I'm coming to the hospital," her father said.

"No, no, you do not have to do that Father." She answered him. She had so much to do. First, Kim needed to go talk to her minister. The plan was Kim would have the minister at Philip's bedside when he woke from surgery. Kim definitely did not want to see her father before she married Philip, because he had a way of getting the truth out of anyone.

The minister agreed to perform the service at Philip's bedside, but he informed Kim he wanted to visit with them both about how serious the vows of marriage are. Kim wished her wedding day could be the kind every girl dreams of, but she knew it was not going to be that way.

When Philip was brought back to his room from surgery, Kim and her minister were waiting. She knew everything was left up to her. Philip woke up when the minister began. He started with a small sermon first. Kim leaned over and whispered, I think we need to say the vows, as Philip needs his rest."

"Oh, of course." The minister started the wedding vows. Kim tightened her grip on Philip's hand when it was his turn to say his vows to her.

The wedding took ten minutes. The two nurses, who stood in as witnesses, left the room. The papers were signed and the minister also left.

Before Philip's eyes slowly closed in sleep, he said, "Thank you, Kim."

She stood at his bedside and her eyes filled with tears, and her thoughts were whirling in her head.

Kim had just married the man who had broken into her car, and then kidnapped her. He had forced her to drive him to the top of a mountain. Her life was in danger all the time she was with him. She was so cold at times she thought she would freeze to death. And minutes ago she had married him. There were so many reasons why she had done this.

The fear of what her father would have done to Philip, came into her thoughts.

Slowly the door opened, and Kim's father stepped into Philip's room with her mother at his side. The three embraced with tears and hugs, talking all at the same time.

When Kim saw how emotional her father was over seeing her, it was at this time she decided what she had done by marrying Philip, was the only way she could have saved him.

He would have never gotten out of jail. Her father would have seen to that, in fact, Kim thought he could have put him on death row.

Kim's father began by saying, "Kim, you need to tell us everything. Do you realize what we were thinking happened to you? We have a large reward for information to find you. This is not like anything you would do."

Her father was doing what he did best.

"Is this the young man you were with? Kim, where and how did you meet him? You haven't told us his name. When did you plan on telling us about him? How could you do this to your mother and brother, who love you like I do?"

"Father! Stop, stop this! I'm not one of your criminals, I'm your daughter. I didn't do anything wrong, except fall in love with a man." Kim shouted back at him.

Kim's mother stood in shocked disbelief. Philip moaned and awoke to hearing Kim's father's loud voice. Everyone turned and stood looking at Philip.

The sheriff's voice was loud and clear, "I know you, I know you, you're Morrison."

"Mom, daddy, this is my husband, Philip." Kim said, with a voice she didn't even recognize. The following five minutes, no one said a word. The quietness in the room was overwhelming.

Kim's mother walked slowly up beside Philip's bed. Philip looked directly into the saddest eyes that were filled with tears. At that moment Philip wanted to confess.

Being the sheriff's wife for so many years had made her very strong. Her husband had been threatened many times and the town had turned against him when he made an unpopular decision, but this time it was her decision. She leaned over and whispered in Philip's ear, and then kissed him on the forehead.

A small little voice in Kim's subconscious mind said, "Mom, this was the only way I could save him from prison, and I know you would have done the same thing."

Kim looked at her father, and it seemed forever until he walked up to Philip's bed, and stood looking at him. Kim went to Philip and reached over and took his hand in hers.

"Philip," the sheriff said deliberately, "I don't know how you did this, but I'm going to find out. In the meantime you're married to my only daughter, and I'm going to be watching you." He turned and took his wife's arm and they walked out of the room.

Philip spoke first, "Kim, I'm so sorry."

"No Philip. We have to make this work, so we can help your brother Will." Kim answered, while feeling unsure.

Philip was hesitating asking her, but he needed her to go see Will. He asked her, "Please, do not tell Will where we have been or what I have done." She agreed, but Kim said, "I'm telling him where you are now, and about your broken leg."

"Kim please, check about the man in the hospital. I know I'm asking you to do a lot. Would you go the hospital and talk to his family?"

Kim was like her mother, a very strong woman, but suddenly she was involved in the most outrageous situation anyone could ever dream up.

Before Kim could help Philip, she had to do something for herself. She had to find her brother Ben, and have a serious talk. Her hands were shaking as she dialed his number. The voice on the other end was totally shocked.

"Kim baby, is that really you? Is it really you? When mom called me, I just couldn't believe you were, well you were alive!"

"Ben, I was never in danger, only on the trip down the mountain. I was never alone. I was with someone I love. Ben, I need you to meet me at the hospital. I'm all right. I would like you to meet my husband." Kim tried to be calm telling him.

Ben laughed and said, "Kim, I thought you said meet my husband?" And he continued to laugh.

"Ben, Ben, that's what I did say." The laughing stopped. Lighthearted he said, "Kim, you have sent this family on a real roller-coaster ride."

"Ben, I really need you, please meet me at the hospital in two hours." Kim begged.

"I'll be there baby sister." Ben reassured her.

CHAPTER 15

Kim's meeting with Will was the assignment Philip had asked her to do. She arrived at the police station feeling nauseated, she knew the sheriff (her father) would be there.

Kim's appearance at the police station was a surprise to her father. They stood looking into each other's eyes. Kim's mind flashed back when she had taken a terrible fall out of a tree in their back yard. He had run to her and lifted her up into his arms and held her close. His large hand gently patted her back and the comfort started immediately.

While Kim was visualizing the comfort she had remembered, she wished she could feel that comfort now, but this was a different time and the circumstances were that her father was suffering too.

She was brought back to reality when her father said, "Kim, what are you doing here?"

"Daddy, I came to see Will, Will Morrison," Kim stated. Her father turned and walked down the hall without saying another word. He stopped in front of a visiting room, and said, "Wait here, Kim."

It took only a few minutes, and Kim heard the door open. A young man stepped in with handcuffs on. On his ankles were shackles. He was just a boy, and he had a lot of features resembling Philip. The look on Will's face was indescribable.

He looked at her and she thought his eyes were pleading to help him. She finally said, "Will, I'm here to talk to you for Philip." Upon hearing Philip's name, he became panicky.

"Where is he? He hasn't been here for two weeks. Where has he been? Why hasn't he come to see me? Has something happened to him?

Kim stood up and walked to him, she leaned down to hug him, when the door opened and her father said," Kim, you cannot touch him." Kim was bent over and she went right ahead and kissed Will on his cheek.

Kim proceeded to tell Will just what Philip wanted him to know. She finished by saying, "Philip will come as soon as he can walk on his broken leg."

Will answered by saying, "Please tell him I need him."

"Will, I have one more thing to tell you, your brother and I are married," Kim said, knowing the response she would get.

Will could only sit and stare at her. Finally, Will broke the silence by saying, "I've never heard Philip talk about you."

She told him, "I know Will, we kept our relationship a secret. You see, my name is Kim Conrad."

The sound of disapproval came from Will's throat. He had recognized the last name. He stood up and moved toward the door. Kim went to him and whispered in his ear, I'm on your side, I'm going to do all I can for you. I'm going to help you, I promise.

Kim put her arms around Will's waist and hugged him, he laid his head down on her shoulder. He needed to know someone cared.

The door opened and the sheriff swiftly stepped in and put his hands between them, making Kim back up.

"Kim, I'm not going to tell you again. Will is a prisoner and you do not touch him, you are not allowed to touch him." The sheriff's voice sounded angry.

The sheriff took Will's arm and pushed him out of the door before Kim could even say good-bye. She left the police station not wanting to deal with her father.

Her tears would not stop as she drove toward the hospital. All she could think about was how young Will was, and she prayed he was telling the truth, that he did not touch Wong Penn Nai. After inquiring at the desk, Kim went to the waiting room and sat quietly, waiting to talk to Wong Penn Nai's family.

A young girl that would fit the description of the family came in and sat across from Kim. Kim started a conversation with her and found she was there visiting her father who had regained consciousness after a severe beating by six boys. She told Kim her father's name was Wong Penn Nai, and was now able to speak five words in Chinese.

Kim needed to know what they were, without sounding like a reporter, Kim asked, "Are the words about the beating?"

"No, the girl said, "He keeps telling my mother how much he loves her." That's great, Kim thought to herself, but it doesn't help us.

When will your father leave the hospital?" Kim asked. The doctor said, "He can go home at the end of the week if he had help at home." the girl answered.

Kim asked, "if he knew the boys that did the beating?" The girl said, "No, you see, it was my brother that the six men wanted." "Your brother knew the men?" Kim needed this information. "Yes, my brother was in big trouble with the men, and my father went in his place." The girl told Kim.

Kim's heart was racing, "Your brother is home now?" Her mind was taking her to this family's home to ask about why the beating took place, and if he could identify four of the six boys involved.

"Yes," the girl said, "He's home in China, my mother sent him home to China, as soon as my father was beaten." Kim's heart nearly stopped. "He is with my grandparents in China," the girl continued.

"Why, why?" Kim asked, "Because," said the girl, "We were afraid they would come back for my brother too."

Kim's voice was getting louder, and the girl was beginning to squirm in her chair. "What was the reason for the beating?" Kim kept up her questions.

The girl was becoming reluctant to answer any more of Kim's probing questions. "My brother was trying to help my parents, they needed money."

Suddenly a small Chinese woman walked in. The girl jumped to her feet and told the lady to sit in her chair, and she would go to her father's room. The elderly lady sat down and her head went down. She immediately closed her eyes.

"I'm sorry about your husband." Kim was very persistent to get more information. In a very soft voice, the elderly lady said, "Thank you, we have so many troubles." Kim was sure Wong Penn Nai's wife was not talking about her husband's beating. She knew what her son was doing to help her and her husband, and she knew it was against the law, or why would they resort to sending him away?

Kim wanted to know more. She told the lady about her brother, Ben, going to China when he was in college. Then she asked, "What part of China did you come from?" The elderly lady had no idea all the information she was telling Kim was for the purpose of helping Will.

The lady described the area in China they came from, and where her parents and son were living. Kim hoped she was telling the truth, because this was too easy.

Kim asked her another question and the old lady got up out of her chair and hurriedly left the room. The question was, could your son identify the four men, and what was he doing for them?

Kim felt uneasy as she left to drive across town to the hospital Philip was in. Something that Mrs. Nai said, lingered in her mind. Mrs. Nai said, "The four men cruel." She had said, "Four men, not six."

CHAPTER 16

Kim walked down the hall, and ahead of her at the nurses' station was Ben. The feeling of happiness, comfort, and peace of mind of mind came over her. He would help, he was always there for her.

The warm greeting was mutual. She took his hand and led him to Philip's room. Ben stood next to Philip's bed shaking his hand

The story came tumbling out of both Philip and Kim. The only part they didn't tell was about the kidnapping. Instead, the story they told Ben was that they had met at a nightclub six months earlier. Of course, why would Ben doubt the story?

After, Kim told Ben of the meeting and conversation she had with Mrs. Nai, and her description of the location her family lived.

Ben said, "I think she either forgot where her parents and son are living, or she didn't want you to know.

"Why Ben, why?" Kim was confused now.

"That area," Ben said, "Is industry, and is next to the huge shipping port of China."

"I must go to the hospital, and get the family to talk to me." Kim was so determined now.

Ben hurried to her side, and said, "You must let me do the leg work I need to find out how long the family has been here, and if they are citizens. We must not overlook one thing. We must not let anyone know we're investigating this family."

Ben went on to say, "The four boys knew they were not beating the son, but they were beating the old man?"

Kim was going to let Ben do what he loved to do. Like their father, he was in police work. He was working hard to open his own private detective office.

Ben woke early the next morning. He recorded the account of all Philip and Kim had told him, making sure he had not forgotten one detail. His first stop was the courthouse. The name Wong Penn Nai was not listed His next stop was the post office, and the family had no home mailing address. What they had was a small coffee shop down town, and it was Ben's guess they lived in the back. He headed for the coffee shop.

The news waiting for Kim when she arrived at the hospital was, Philip was released and could go home, after the doctor checked him.

Kim made a phone call to the one person who loved her unconditionally, her mother. She asked if she could come to her home and take care of Philip. Kim felt Ben could use her help.

Ben's arrival at the cafe took a surprising turn of events. The sign in the window read, "Help Wanted." Ben decided Kim would make a good waitress. Kim received his call and whispered to Philip, about the plan Ben had for her.

When Kim had Philip safely settled in, with her mother watching over him, she left to apply for a job she knew nothing about. Kim's application stated her name was Kim Collins. They definitely would not hire her if she had used the sheriff's last name. She also could not use her married name of Morrison.

The first day Kim only asked questions about her job. The second day, she began asking all the questions Ben told her to ask.

She found the cook loved to talk, so any spare time Kim had, she was in the kitchen with the cook. He told her Wong Penn Nai's son had suddenly disappeared after his father was beaten.

Kim said, "Yes, I know he's home in China."

"No, he not from China, he from Laos." Kim's heart felt like it was beating faster, but she could not let on she cared one way or the other about this family. What she really wanted right then was to tell Ben.

The questions continued whenever she had a break. Kim asked, "Why would anyone beat an old man?"

"He owed money, he owed boss money." The cook told her.

"For what," Kim asked, did he owe money? "He was making money for the owner, working for him." Kim knew he could tell her all she wanted to know, but she had to be very discreet so he would not suspect her.

Kim nonchalantly asked the cook again. "What did he owe the money for?"

"Boss bring family here, son steal money. Can't talk, have to work." And turned his back on her.

Kim wanted to scream, "No, tell me everything you know."

Kim was excited to tell Philip and Ben all she had learned when she got home. Her mother and Philip had gotten along extremely well. After her mother fixed their supper, she left for her home.

The three of them sat at the table discussing what they would do next. Ben repeated everything they knew so far. Then he said, "I need to go to the hospital and see if the Nai family members each have a green card. If they have one we know it is fake. Also, I'll go to the waiting room and see if I can get the family to talk to me."

"Kim," Ben said, "You must find out if the boss has brought more families to the United States from Laos. You must be very careful, the owner is, well, we know how dangerous he is."

After Ben left, Kim got Philip upon his crutches and helped him into the bathroom to prepare for bed. She got out his new pajamas and scissors. Kim cut off one leg to fit over his cast. It was agreed, by them both, the honeymoon would wait until this situation was behind them, and Will would be free. Philip promised her he would court her first, before they went on a honeymoon.

The next day's information was almost frightening. They met again at Kim's house. Ben told how he had talked a nurse into getting Mrs. Nai's green card and secretly letting him see it. He also talked the nurse into making a copy of it, before giving it back to her. The nurse told Mrs. Nai it was for the insurance co.

Kim's report was what Ben had been thinking all along, but had not told them. The owner was bringing people into the United States at a very high price. The cook was telling her everything he knew.

Kim pressured the cook to tell her what he thought Wong Penn Nai's son had done.

"Son not smart." he said. "He working off money of parents and sister coming here. He gets the money from the ship's Captain and take to boss. He steal money. Boss sent four boys to teach lesson. Beat wrong man."

"If he was working for his parents passage here, what money are you talking about?" Kim needed him to say what Ben suspected. "How does the boss get the people here, on what ship?"

"Talk later, talk later," the cook replied.

That night, Ben said, "I think it's time to tell the sheriff, and get his help before one of us gets hurts.

The cook could get into trouble talking with you so much if someone sees you."

The plan they made, Ben would take all the information with him to the police station, and Kim would work in the càfe one more day. Philip firmly objected to Kim going one more day to the cafe. He no longer wanted her involved for fear of her coming in contact with the boss. Kim begged Philip to, "Understand they were doing this for Will."

The first time Ben sat down with the sheriff, and discussed this criminal underworld activity, the sheriff wanted to believe Ben. He told Ben, "Four of the six men being held would not talk. They never say one word, they just sit and stare."

Ben said, "Dad, they fear for their lives. Even in jail they are not safe. The boss is dangerously vicious."

After the sheriff heard the story and got all of Ben's information, he removed Will and his friend from the cell with the four men. He was beginning to have doubts about Will's involvement. What they needed now was the proof.

The investigation started in full swing. The sheriff decided against pulling the cook in for questioning, because he could be killed over it.

For Kim, the day started as usual, except when the door of the cafe opened and several men dressed in dark suits entered. The closed sign was put on the front door. Only a few employees were left to work, the rest were sent home.

Everyone working there hurried and set up a table in the back room against a wall. Kim tried to keep busy while watching what was happening.

When the table was ready, one man stepped outside and escorted a big, dark haired man in. He was dressed in a black suit, black coat, black hat, with a red scarf around his neck. He stood tall and straight, his build was statue-like. He had a ring on each finger, they were large diamonds in all shapes. His fingernails were all manicured, and his skin looked soft and completely flawless.

Kim went to the kitchen quickly to ask about this man. Cook said, "Can't talk, can't talk he boss, he boss. Must cook good for him."

From there Kim went into the bathroom, she called Ben on her cell phone, and flushed the stool at the same time so no one would over hear her. She told him, "He could not come into the cafe till the boss was done eating."

Ben told her, "I'll be outside waiting with the sheriff and my camera. We cannot do anything today. We need to know about his ship, and we need proof of what he's doing.

The boss and his men had a special dinner. He did the talking while his men sat and listened intently. Kim could not hear any of the conversation, because she stayed away from the table. She did not want be seen.

After nearly two hours, the boss stood up. One of his men went out of the door to make sure it was safe for his boss to go out, then the driver pulled the limousine in front of the cafe.

Kim went back to the bathroom to call Ben, and inform him, the boss and his men were coming out.

As Kim stepped out of the bathroom, she stepped right in front of the boss as he was walking toward the kitchen to thank the cook. Their eyes met in a cold inquisitive stare. Kim tried to talk, she opened her mouth, but nothing came out.

The words she heard came from the boss. "I'm sorry miss, did I frighten you?"

"No, oh no, I'm in your way, please excuse me." Kim managed to say. She wanted and tried to move around him, when his hand reached out, and he said, "I don't think we've met." Kim was hoping he couldn't see the sweat beads coming out on her face, and her face suddenly felt flushed. Now he wanted to shake her hand, and it was feeling cold and clammy. He took her hand and raised it up to his face and kissed the back of her hand.

CHAPTER 17

Kim felt frozen in time. His lips remained on her hand for what seemed forever. She knew she was going to have to tell him her name so she could get away from him.

"Kim, my name is Kim Collins. I do hope your dinner was satisfactory to you." Kim said, trying to keep the conversation impersonal, and trying to keep her voice from sounding nervous.

"Kim, my name is Hundraayus, and I'd like to invite you to my home for dinner on Saturday evening. Where can I send my limousine for you?" His eyes were glued to her. Suddenly the feeling she had when she discovered Philip in her car returned. What did Hundraayus want with her?

Immediately Kim prayed the floor under her would open up and she could slip down into the basement. Hundraayus' bodyguards were standing on each side of him, and their eyes felt like they were penetrating her brain.

She needed to say something, but what? In a second Kim made the decision, because she had no choice. She worked to get her voice to sound like she would be honored to dine with him.

"Yes, I would be honored," Kim managed to fool him. "Would you mind if I drove to your home, as my neighbors are very snoopy." She said struggling, because she owned her house and if he looked up her address, he would know she lied about her name, and he would find out she was the sheriff's daughter.

Her body began to tremble as she waited for his answer. Then she heard him say, "I'll draw you a map, because my home is up in the mountains. Perhaps it would be wise for you to stay overnight as the road is narrow in places, and traveling down the mountain would not be safe for a young woman at night."

Kim knew she had to agree with everything he was saying. She accepted the invitation and the map, and then excused herself to help finish her work so she could go home.

Kim helped clear the table Hundraayus and his men had eaten at. She was looking for a clue of any kind and she found it under the table. It was book matches. On it was an advertisement of a shipping line.

She had learned from Ben how to make sure no one was following her by making several stops. It took an extra hour, and Philip was waiting at the door on his crutches. She slipped her arms around his waist and hugged him until she felt safe and secure.

They all had their usual meeting, but this time it included the sheriff.

Kim began, and told them every detail. She showed them the book matches she had found. Now they had something to go on. Ben told them the pictures he had taken of the men coming out of the cafe were being developed as they talked.

The sheriff said. "I watched the men through my binoculars as they left the cafe. I believe the boss is running his business from his home, and his men are doing the dirty work because I have never seen the boss before."

Each one studied the map. The sheriff explained how they would start, "I'll start a surveillance team on the boss's house, and I'll send my men down to the pier on a stakeout to watch who leaves his ships. We need evidence to be able to search his ships.

The reactions from Kim's father, brother, and especially Philip were all the same. They would not allow her to go for dinner on Saturday night.

Philip had been strangely quiet until everyone left. Then he said, "Why did this man ask you to supper, when he did not even know you?"

"Philip, I knew he was looking and watching me while I worked, but I tried to keep away from him. Please Philip, I did not do anything to make him notice me." Kim said, feeling terrible for Philip.

"Kim, you are so beautiful," Philip told her for the first time. Why wouldn't he notice you? But you have to realize this man is so very cruel and uncaring who he hurts."

"Philip," she said, in a voice that sounded like she was begging. "My father is going to stop him from hurting anyone else, and prove Will did not take part in the beating."

"Kim, I believe the only way we can prove Will was not one of the men committing the crime is to bring back to this country Wong Penn Nai's son. He needs to be a witness against Hundraayus. He needs to tell us all of the crimes connected to Hundraayus' unlawful proceedings," Philip confided in her and sounded sure of himself.

"Philip, how can we get Mr. Nai's son back?" Kim was almost afraid to ask. He looked at her and said, "I'm going to Laos, and bring him back."

Kim was sure Philip had made up his mind to go. "No, she said, "We need to tell father and Ben first." She knew she had to convince him.

"If you're so determined someone should go. Please let Ben go instead. He has a license to carry a gun for protection. Also

Philip, you have a cast on your leg which could be a big problem, so I'll go with Ben."

This was not the first time Philip had been in a desperate situation and had acted irrational. Only this time he had Kim on his side instead of against him. She was trying to keep the situation within the realm of the law, and not let this get out of control.

Kim decided to stay home and spend the day with Philip, as she had been so busy lately. She could tell he needed her attention and to know of her loyalty to him.

Kim called the cafe and asked for the cook. She explained she would not be in today, and he told her the boss had called and questioned him about her. Where she came from, where she lived. Why a beautiful, well-educated woman, was working in a cafe.?

The cook went on to say, "I told him that I don't know anything about you." Then he added, "Missy, you know, be careful, this man mean, always gets what he wants." Before Kim hung up, she thanked him and asked that he not say anything to anyone about her.

That evening's meeting was loud and emotional. First, Philip expressed how important it was for Wong Penn Nai's son to be returned, and asked to testify against Hundraayus. The sheriff said, "We must offer him asylum and safeguard him against Hundraayus. The sanction we offer him will come from me."

The sheriff opened his mouth to say something else, and Philip interrupted, saying, I forbid Kim to go after him." Everyone turned and looked at him. Kim was suddenly feeling an intense affection for him. As far as Kim's father was concerned, Philip had just said the right thing.

Ben immediately offered to go, and Philip said, "I'm the one who needs to go. I'll leave as soon as I can get a ticket." He just got up and left the room.

"Please, daddy," Kim pleaded, "Go to him and explain this trip could be dangerous for him. Tell him his cast would be a hindrance to him. He is still taking pain medicine. Tell him Ben is trained in this type of surroundings, because Philip will not allow me to go, you must send one of your best men with Ben."

The sheriff listened and then said to his daughter, "Philip is right, you must not go, he must not go. Ben will have the law on his side to go to Laos and bring back this man. Ben will have my sanction. I know just who will go with him and help find our witness. This is an opportunity for us to stop a criminal from destroying people's lives. From taking money from people who are destitute. From sending his henchmen to beat an old man."

CHAPTER 18

The sheriff was becoming more determined to stop Hundraayus. The phone rang as the sheriff was telling Kim his plan.

The officer on the other end was very excited, he was one of the men watching Hundraayus' ship. He told the sheriff they witnessed families leaving the ship, their physical condition looked in need of a doctor, food, and their clothing was very dirty.

Families, with little children, struggled down the gangplank in the dark, looking tired and hungry. The children were crying, the mothers sobbing, holding on to their husbands.

These people had paid Hundraayus their life savings to get here. Now they had no money and no place to live. They probably would live in poverty for a long time, and because they were not citizens, they would live hiding from the law, instead of being protected by the law.

This is the reason they all went to Hundraayus' manufacturing plant, and could live in rooms in the back or upstairs. And everyone lived in fear of the man that had promised them freedom and yet treated them so badly.

Before they were allowed to leave the ship, the Captain warned them they could not talk to anyone. Their life of drudgery was about to start.

CHAPTER 19

Ben boarded the plane, and sat next to the window. He was thinking about all the instructions his father had given him. About sneaking into Laos, and sneaking out with a man that was in hiding. The policemen, who had watched Hundraayus' ship and his home, had met with Ben and told him what they knew about the man and his operations.

A beautiful oriental woman slipped into the seat beside him. He turned his head and glanced at her. Within seconds he recognized her. He had seen her at the police station at different times. She was a woman men always took a second look at.

She leaned toward Ben and said, "Hello, my name is Cynthia, and I'm your partner." Cynthia had been with the police department for nearly five years. She had worked her way to a private detective, with her own office.

This came as a complete surprise to Ben. He was expecting to work with one of the big burly men on the force. Ben's father thought that the two of them would look like a couple on their honeymoon.

Cynthia was a perfectionist. She insisted Ben tell her every detail. The questions were endless. Ben enjoyed looking at her, but in the pit of his stomach he was angry. Finally, he said, "Why you?"

"Because, I'm going to cover your skinny little ass." Cynthia answered him. This was his first warning he had met his match.

Cynthia was resilient, and could withstand difficult situations, and this could possibly turn out to be a difficult situation.

The next few hours neither one spoke. Finally, Cynthia said, "Ben, I realize you would have preferred a large, macho, long-haired, bearded, plainclothes, tobacco-chewing, detective, but you're going to have to put your faith in me, I'll do my very best for you."

Ben felt he was being pressured into saying something nice that he didn't want to say. So, he firmly said, "Lets do what we came to do."

The Captain interrupted their spirited conversation.

After they landed, Ben tried to get ahead of her by moving swiftly. He grabbed his bag and stepped out to the curb. Cynthia was right beside him. He didn't know Cynthia's background. She had grown up in a family of karate champions. Before this trip was over, Ben would find out all about Cynthia.

The cab was small and cramped. Cynthia gave the cabby the name of the hotel, in Laotian, which Ben could not understand. Ben was determined not to let her get ahead of him. He was a professional, he lifted his arm and slipped it around her shoulder. Without realizing her body was doing it, she stiffened up.

The streets were narrow and very crowded. It took nearly two hours to get where they would be staying. Bicycle riders rode in the middle of the street. An American was always spotted and stared at. Ben and Cynthia did not talk for fear the taxi driver could understand English.

The driver pulled the taxi up in front of a worn-out, dark and dirty building that they called a hotel. On entering the lobby, a bad feeling came over both of them. The clerk looked at them suspiciously. Ben pulled Cynthia to him and kissed her firmly on her mouth. Her first reaction was to slap him, raise her knee and hurt him badly.

Being undercover, a detective did what ever he had to, and Ben was playing his part, Cynthia wondered why he had to play his part so well.

The clerk took them up two flights of stairs and down a dirty hall that had no rug on it. The boards squeaked as they walked to their room. Doors opened and people peeked out at them. Ben walked very close to her, he was the one they were looking at.

They stepped inside their room and found one bed, and one chair, a small wooden box to set their bags on. The room was not clean, and Cynthia wondered if the bedding had been changed recently.

Ben had already made up his mind, he was not sleeping on anything but the bed. Cynthia looked at the bed and decided to sleep in her clothes. She wished she could forget about the kiss they shared. Because she knew it meant nothing to him.

Cynthia pulled back the covers making sure she was under the top sheet and Ben lay on top on the top sheet. It was nearly twenty-four hours since they had left home and they were both exhausted. She waited till she heard Ben breathing heavy, then relaxed and dropped off to sleep.

Ben awoke first and when he moved, Cynthia was up and setting on the edge of the bed. Ben whispered in her ear, they would talk when they were outside, where no one could hear them.

They each used the bathroom that was on the first floor. They dipped water from a large pail that looked as if it had not been cleaned for a long time. The washbasin was used by everyone. Each person used it and just dumped it out. They did not remain in the bathroom long for the smell was so unpleasant.

The bags they carried had straps that could be used as backpacks. Nothing was left in the room, for they trusted no one.

CHAPTER 20

Out on the street, the aroma was heavy from vendors with food, vegetables, and fruit, but animal odor was present also. Dogs were running loose through the street. Weary looking women sat on the dirty streets with a canvas in front of them holding their vegetables, fruit, and rice products. These people owned nothing, the small amount of money they made only provided them enough to continue to live.

People turned and stared at him. It was her turn to pretend. She slipped her arm around his waist, so people would understand they were together. The noise was so loud. People darted here and there, they all appeared to talk at the same time, and the dogs barked loudly from hunger.

They walked a short distance when the clouds moved in. It was a downpour, this was the rainy season. The streets turned into mud. Walking was the only way to get through the crowded street now. It was humid, so the rain was warm. Ben tried to find some cover for them. While Cynthia was getting her small umbrella out, he found a shed that was holding pigs, so they stood under a ledge, but the odor was horrendous.

Ben looked down at his boots, they were covered with mud and animal waste. His eyes moved and stopped at the sight of Cynthia's pant-cuffs and boots. Her boots were expensive leather. Now they were ruined. Cynthia opened her umbrella, and held it up for Ben to get under, he moved close to her. They stood very close, aware of each other's bodies. Ben thought how tough she could act, but her body was so soft.

When the rain finally stopped, they continued to stop at each hut, and Cynthia would ask about the Wong Penn Nai's family.

It was decided by them both, no one was going to tell them anything if they didn't tell them something, such as the family was related to Cynthia. Ben mentioned they should bring fruit to each family, so they wouldn't be so suspicious.

They needed to return to their hotel before it got dark. Walking as fast as they could, because they knew they were not welcome here. They would start again in the morning.

Ben was wishing they had started back to town sooner. The clouds were still overhead, so darkness was already upon them, and it was starting to rain again. The Laotian families had left their rice fields and hurried to their huts.

Ben and Cynthia were nearly to their hotel. They were both having a hard time with the heavy mud caked on their boots. Cynthia stopped to scrape her boots.

Suddenly Ben was jumped from behind, and knocked to the ground. The second man grabbed Ben's backpack. Cynthia turned to see a man with a knife in his hand leaning over Ben. Cynthia dropped her backpack so she had the strap in her hand, she swung the backpack hard at the man, knocking the knife out of his hand and knocking him away from Ben.

Ben jumped to his feet as the second man was about to hit Cynthia. She raised her leg kicking the man in the chest, and especially the heart area. He landed hard on his back. The first man tried to get up, Ben was on top on him. Ben hit him only once and the man was out. Ben quickly picked up his backpack and the knife.

Ben yelled at Cynthia, "Lets go!" They moved away from the crowd that had gathered and were chanting, "Kill 'em, kill' em," in Laotian.

When they went through the hotel door, they took the stairs two at a time. Cynthia slammed the door of their room behind them. Ben pushed the bed over in front of the door, then they sat on the bed to get their breath.

Cynthia spoke first, "Do you realize how close you came to being killed? Do you know what that crowd was saying?" Ben sat for a minute looking at her, yet not even seeing her. He thought it had to be robbery, no one knew who they were, or what they were doing there.

The knock on the door sent chills into both of them. Ben pulled the bed away from the door just enough to see a small boy. He was dirty, his clothes were dirty. He was wearing an old worn-out stocking cap, and he looked like one of the many homeless children they had seen on the street.

Ben stepped back so Cynthia could see him. The boy told Cynthia he had witnessed the fight, and he had seen Ben drop his badge. The boy said, "I picked it up and hid it. I followed you here." Cynthia asked him his name, but he refused to tell her.

Ben wished he could understand what they were saying. Ben started telling Cynthia what to ask him. "Ask about the Wong Penn Nai's family. Do you live in this area? Can he show us the way? Do we need to hire a driver? Tell him we'll give him money, if he can tell us anything. Tell him he must not tell anyone about us."

Cynthia asked everything Ben had instructed her to say. Then she very firmly told the boy, "You must not tell this to anyone."

The boy continued to talk, he kept repeating something, Ben told Cynthia to tell the boy he could stay in the room with them. They had to make sure he did not tell anyone. Cynthia explained to the boy what Ben had said. The boy continued repeating the words. He was getting louder and louder.

Finally Cynthia stopped him, and turned to Ben and said, "He will only help us if we take him to America with us." Ben could not even imagine touching this filthy little boy, let alone taking him home with them.

Ben took a few steps away from the boy, Cynthia followed. They discussed the predicament they were in, and what to do about it.

Cynthia said, "We have no choice, we have come a long way to get stopped now. We have to tell him we'll try to take him home with us."

Ben was silent as Cynthia went to this little street urchin, and told him, "We'll do everything we can to take you to America." The little boy talked and talked, until Cynthia told him they all had to sleep. He was smiling as he lay down on the floor on a blanket Cynthia had given him off of the bed. He did not remove his cap, he pulled it down over his ears.

Ben awoke to hear Cynthia talking to the boy. She was trying to tell the boy he must go to the bathroom with Ben, not her. The boy's voice was getting emotional, and Cynthia thought he was going to cry. She finally suggested she take him to the bathroom and she would stand outside the bathroom door, then walk him back to their room.

After they met back in the room, it was very clear, the boy had not washed one speck of dirt off of himself, nor was he going to.

The boy spoke only in Laotian to Cynthia, "I'll take you out of Pay Lay through the back streets and alleys to keep you safe. I'll take you to the village of the people you are looking for. Then I'm going to America with you, right?" Cynthia answered him saying, "After we find this family, we'll talk about you're going back with us."

The little boy was so anxious to start, he was the first one out of the door. He told Cynthia, "We need to go out while it's still dark." They hurried to get into the alley. The boy was always ahead of them. He knew exactly where he was going. He suddenly stopped, he was gently lifting the lid off of a garbage can. He leaned deep in the can, and the only thing showing was his tiny little legs and feet.

Within inches of his body, Cynthia and Ben watched in terror as two large rats jumped out of the can. It was so terrifying for them to see, and the little boy continued picking out food. He was picking as fast as he could It was scraps, bits, and pieces of discarded food off of plates from a restaurant. He stuffed the food in his coat pocket. Before he finished, four other children were there, fighting him for the food.

Ben separated them and pulled him away. It didn't make any difference, they continued to tear at the little boy's coat. Ben picked him up and walked away from the other children. He put him down and hadn't even thought about not wanting to touch him.

Cynthia found a Laotian woman selling fruit on a street comer. She purchased enough for all of them, also enough to give some to the Wong Penn Nai's family. If and when they found them.

They left the town, and found they were again in the rice fields. The little boy was ahead, running and looking at all of the rice farmers. The search went on until Ben thought they needed to start back. His memory of the night before was still very fresh in his mind.

Without any warning, the little boy darted into a rice paddy, and started talking to a young man. The young man turned and looked at Ben and Cynthia. He started to run in the opposite direction. The little boy reacted at the same time, he ran a few steps, leaped, and grabbed the man around his legs, and they both fell in the water. Ben was there on top of both of them. The little boy came up coughing and choking.

Cynthia was trying to talk to the young man. "Are you Wong Penn Nai's son? Your parents need you to come back to America, to clear their name, so Hundraayus will not hurt them. You need to do the honorable thing and return to America, and help your parents." Cynthia was trying to make him feel guilty for leaving them. The man's eyes looked wild, he quickly looked back and forth from Ben to Cynthia.

Ben tried next saying, "Your mother, father, and sister are in danger when they leave the hospital. Don't you understand that? Hundraayus knows they know all about his business that is forbidden by the law, and if he is caught, could go to prison."

The young man finally spoke in half English, and half Laotian, "My parents are not safe, and my grandparents are not safe." His voice began to crack making it more difficult to understand him.

Ben interrupted him saying, "You, and your family will be protected by the law, I promise, as my father is the sheriff in the city your parents and sister are living."

The young man was still not convinced, he was not ready to trust anyone. Ben told him, "Sheriff Conrad sends his sanctions to you, from the time we found you, till Hundraayus goes to jail, he will take care of you and your family. You must take us to your grandparents, and because, it's nearly dark out, it is not safe for us to walk back into the city."

CHAPTER 21

Finally, Shu Lee Nai agreed to take Ben and Cynthia to see his grandparents.

Cynthia looked around, and the little boy was not with them. It was completely dark now, and they had no way to look for him. He had slipped away unnoticed, and did not tell them.

Shu Lee Nai hurried along in front of them, walking on narrow paths around the rice paddies. Ben and Cynthia had to keep up, for they had no light at all. They both noticed the path was getting steeper. To Cynthia the path was going straight up, it was as if they were climbing a cliff.

Shu Lee Nai stopped and said, "Stay here." Then he was gone. Cynthia moved close enough so her arm was touching Ben. The only sound was their breathing. Ben leaned over and whispered in Cynthia's ear, "What if he doesn't come back?" She tried not to think about that. Cynthia felt Ben touch her arm, then he pulled her to sit down. Within minutes the rain poured down on them, and because, it was a cool evening, it felt cold to them both. She reached in her backpack and opened her umbrella. It kept the rain off, but did not stop them from shivering.

Cynthia whispered, "I'll be glad when we're back home, where I can shower. Where I can go to my closet, and pick out a different set of clothes each day, with matching shoes. Where I can eat whatever I want, not just rice. Where I can turn the lights on, watch television, or read a book at night." She was about to mention the new home she had just purchased, when Shu Lee

Nai said, "You can come now." Neither one had even heard him return.

They jumped to their feet and tried to keep up with his fast small steps. He stopped, and told them to, "Bend down." They were entering a cave. The only light was from a lantern. They were out of the rain, but it felt damp and cool inside. Ben and Cynthia could not stand up, only a small child could stand in it, so they both got down on their knees.

Sitting on a blanket on the dirt floor were two old people. Shu Lee's grandparents. They both looked old and wrinkled, they were sitting bent over. They looked gaunt from malnutrition, rice was their main source of food. They were dirty, as was their torn clothing. What little sunlight they received was when they sat in the small opening of the cave. Shu Lee was keeping them hidden from Hundraayus.

He began to explain to Ben and Cynthia what happened to make his old grandparents live in this squalid condition. He said, "My father, Wong Penn Nai was a fisherman. He had his own boat, and each day he fished from early morning till he filled his boat's hold. He would pack his fish into boxes to be shipped to the United States."

At this time Hundraayus' name was brought into the conversation, and Shu Lee said his name with a noticeable dislike, Hundraayus sent his men to approach and pressure Shu Lee to pack drugs in the boxes of fish. The boxes of fish were then put on Hundraayus' ship.

Hundraayus promised Shu Lee, he could take all of his family, including his grandparents to the United States if he would permit and commit this crime for one year. Then his father must sell his fishing business to someone who would continue the same procedure. The money his father received for his business would all go to Hundraayus to take him and his family to America.

The first ship was full, the room in the bottom of the ship was very small, and it was crowded, so the grandparents were told they would have to wait for the next ship. They knew about Hundraayus, and they knew they would be illegal aliens, so they were a threat to Hundraayus.

Shu Lee acted as if he needed to tell this story. At this point, he wanted to tell the miserable part about his father's beating that he should have received. The trip to the United States, he described as horrendous. The room was only six foot by nine foot in size. It was packed with human bodies. Bathroom privileges were immoral. Food was passed through the door once a day. The people made sure everyone had their share before anyone could take a bite. The ship had it's own doctor, and if someone became ill, he would go to the room, and treat them only if they were extremely sick. Shu Lee was pouring his heart out.

Cynthia was listening and memorizing every word, but for a moment her attention was drawn toward what she was sure was a movement behind Shu Lee's grandparents. She strained to see if it would move again. It didn't. So she quickly turned her attention back to Shu Lee.

He was saying, "Hundraayus took all of my father's money, and made us work for nothing. I was watching that night my father was beaten. My father made me hide when he saw the men coming toward us".

Ben interrupted him saying, "You saw the men? You saw their faces?"

Shu Lee answered slowly, "Yes, yes, I saw the four men who did the beating."

Ben repeated Shu Lee's answer. "Four men, but six men were there."

"Yes," Shu Lee said. "But only four of the men did the beating." Ben kept pressuring him, "Six men were arrested, why didn't you tell the police?"

"Because my mother insisted I leave the country immediately." he answered defensively.

Cynthia's voice sounded angry when she asked, "What did you do, Shu Lee to cause all of this trouble?" Shu Lee looked at Cynthia and said, "I took back the exact amount of money that Hundraayus' men stole from my father."

Shu Lee explained, "When I arrived back home, my friend brought my grandparents here. Hundraayus' men have looked everywhere for them. I have gotten my family in so much trouble, Hundraayus wants to kill us all."

Ben repeated what he had told him earlier, "We must get you, and your grandparents back to the United States to save the rest of your family."

Shu Lee shook his head and said, "That seems so impossible, look how dirty they are, look at the only clothes they have. They have been in this cave so long they can hardly walk."

Ben and Cynthia began to talk to each other, they were sure they could do this. The grandparents could each wear a set of their clothing. Ben would slip back into town, and call his father. They would all need tickets for a plane ride to America.

When Ben told the plan to Shu Lee, he got very excited, and said, "No, no, you must not go, my little friend must go. It is a holiday in the city, many authorities will be there. People would look at a white man."

Shu Lee crawled to the area behind his grandparents, he was talking to someone. Shu Lee crawled back to where he had been sitting, and walking behind him was the same little boy that had spent a night with them, and then suddenly disappeared, when they were talking to Shu Lee at the rice field. Shu Lee's little friend told Ben, "I'll do what ever you want me to do."

Ben had a very uneasy feeling giving this child such a dangerously unsafe task.

"First," Ben said, "What is your name?" The child stood and didn't answer for what seemed a very long time. Then in a quiet soft voice, said, "Shunlu. My name is Shunlu."

"What about your parents?" Ben asked,

"I'm alone, my mother and father died in a bombing, I stay here with Shu Lee," the child answered, then added. "I want to go to America with him." Cynthia listened, and something bothered her about that name.

Shunlu went to the small opening and looked out into the night. It would be dark for a few more hours. Shunlu needed to get started now. Ben needed to talk fast so not to waste any darkness of the night.

He begged the child to, "Hide if you think someone is following you. Go to the American Embassy in Pay Lay, and ask for help, give them my card. Tell them they need to call my father, Sheriff Conrad, you need to tell the sheriff the whole story."

Ben warned the child again when he was crawling through the cave opening, "You must not let anyone get a hold of my name card, if by chance, you're stopped by a stranger, you must tear it up. You must put it in your mouth and chew on it so no one, can read it. If the police stop you before you get to the Embassy, you must do the same thing, because we cannot trust anyone. Hundraayus is a very powerful man. He has a lot of connections in this country."

Each time Shunlu left the cave, he always climbed down the cliff a different way so he would not leave a track. He left the cave every night, and tried to get to all of the garbage cans behind the eating places before any other scavengers. He would do the same thing this night, hide the food, and pick it up after he had done what Ben had asked him to do. He would take the food back to the cave to feed She Lee's grandparents. This night he had to bring more food back, because the only food in the cave was cold rice.

He was running faster than he had ever run before. He ran along the paths next to the rice paddies, then on into the city, and through the alleys. He pulled the same bag out of his coat that he used every night. He filled the bag with food, it smelled fresher tonight, it was the bread that was stale. He found a place to hide his bag, and covered it with boxes.

Behind him was a noise, he turned to see two men hurrying toward him. He started darting in and out of the buildings, and market places.

It was just getting light out when Shunlu arrived at the American Embassy. He hid in some bushes next to the gate, realizing he could not go through the front security entrance. He looked for a tree that had branches hanging close to the fence. Shunlu would have to climb out to the end, and jump over the high fence.

He crawled along under the bushes, and then climbed up the tree. He got out as far as he could. The limb was beginning to bend down. Shunlu leaped over the fence, and was inside. He ran to the building and was sneaking along the building, heading to the back door. He got to the door, reached up, and turned the knob. Shunlu pushed with all of his strength, the door opened just enough for his small body to squeeze in. His goal was to find the door with the name Ambassador on it.

He was in a hall, and it smelled so good as he was extremely hungry. Crouching down, he slipped into the kitchen. It was full of cooks talking and laughing. He quickly crawled under a table, it was now that he was feeling frightened.

When the voices stopped, he peeked out and found he was alone in the kitchen. Shunlu crept out and hurried through the kitchen and down a hall.

He heard footsteps coming, the door he opened and stepped into was a closet. It was so dark so he stood like a statue, he didn't want to knock anything over and make a noise. The footsteps went by the door. He waited, then opened the door slowly and stepped out.

"Ambassador, Ambassador," Shunlu had said it over and over until he had memorized the letters. He went by two doors, the name on the door was not Ambassador, so he almost ran to the next door. It had the right letters. His little hand twisted the knob, the door opened, Shunlu was in. His hand reached back and closed the door.

The large man sitting behind the desk, looked up, and his mouth opened up in complete shock. He yelled, "Someone get in here now."

In seconds the office was filled with stern looking men, all wearing black suits. Shunlu ran to his side, holding Ben's card, "Please mister, you have to call Ben's father, Sheriff Conrad, in America, we need his help." Shunlu was pleading, with tears running down his cheeks. The dirt on his face was also running and smearing, making him look worse.

The Ambassador held his hand in the air to stop his reinforcements. He took the card from Shunlu, studied it closely.

Then the card was passed around to each man. Shunlu began to tell his story.

No one spoke till the little boy was quiet. The Ambassador picked up the phone and dialed the number.

He asked for Sheriff Conrad. It took a few minutes. Then Sheriff Conrad answered, and was told that his son was asking for help. Ben, Cynthia, Shu Lee, his grandparents, and now a little boy, called Shunlu were added to the list, to get out of Laos.

The discussion that followed was about how they could help Ben and his partner to the Embassy. With all of their responsibilities, and Hundraayus looking for them, it was going to be very difficult. There was no one in the whole world that was happier at this time than Shunlu. He jumped up and down clapping his little hands. He was going to America.

The job he had to do first was to get all of his friends that were hiding in the cave to the Embassy without Hundraayus' men seeing them. Shunlu told the Ambassador he would bring one person at a time during the night. If everything went well he could make two trips a night.

He told the men in the office, "I must leave now as I have food hidden, and I must get it back to them. The men stood and looked at each other and one spoke saying, "Our cook will pack food for you. You must not go into the alley where you saw the two men. Stay out of the usual places and alleys. "Two of the men carried Shunlu out of the front gate hidden in a cardboard box. When they got to the bushes, they set the box under a bush and went back through the gate. Shunlu waited for a little while, and then crawled out carrying his sack of food. He was returning to the cave, while making sure no one was following him. He went straight to the rice field first, because he knew Shu Lee would be there.

Shunlu told him what the plan was, and how Sheriff Conrad was going to help. Everyone in the area was working in the rice paddies, so Shunlu went to the cave. He crawled along the cliff, and up into the opening.

CHAPTER 23

Ben and Cynthia were extremely happy to see him. Regardless of how dirty he was, or how badly he smelled, they both hugged him. The food was eaten instantly. Shunlu explained the plan on how they would get to the American Embassy.

After they had talked of the long trip for the grandparents, Ben said to Shunlu, "I need to go with you, to help with the old couple."

The day was long waiting for evening to come. When there was no light out at all, Shunlu told the grandmother where he and Ben were taking her, and why. They crawled out of the cave, one at a time. Ben then picked her up and with Shunlu in front, they made their way down the cliff. Ben thought if he dropped her or if he fell with her, she would break, as she was so fragile.

Shunlu. was used to running fast, he found he would have to stop and go back, and wait till Ben caught up. Ben was hurrying along when he thought he heard voices. He stopped and listened Just then Shunlu was at his side. Whispering, they decided they must go through the rice fields, to keep away from the men that were looking for them.

The mud Ben went through made his legs feel pain he had never felt before. The old woman clung to him. Ben told Shunlu, "We must get everyone to the Embassy tonight. Hundraayus is getting too close."

As soon as they got to the Embassy, the Ambassador's men were watching, and at the gate, waiting. They took the woman from Ben, and Ben told them "Shunlu and I are going back to get the rest."

The trip back was faster. Ben tried to keep up with Shunlu. Shunlu whistled as they got to the opening. He was alerting Shu Lee that they were back. Ben and Shunlu stood quietly a few feet from the cave opening. The answering whistle was loud and clear. Ben crawled in first with Shunlu following. They all tried to talk at the same time until Ben raised his voice and commanded everyone to, "Get ready to leave now, we must hurry. You cannot take anything with you."

It was at this time Ben explained, "We have to stay off of the paths, that means we have to walk through the rice fields to keep away from Hundraayus' men,"

Crawling out of the cave was the easy part, going down the incline in the dark was the hard part. Each one was scared of falling, and hurting the next in line. Ben was carrying grandfather as he stepped into the rice paddy water and sank up to his knees.

Shunlu was first, he knew the area best, Cynthia was next, then Shu Lee, in case Ben needed help with his grandfather. The cold watery mud stuck to their feet and pants, making their bodies shiver. They all tried to make as little noise as possible, but that was almost impossible, because they had to lift their feet and legs out of the water and the mud clung to their shoes, and then would drop off, back into the water making a splashing noise.

The water was up to Shunlu's hips, at times slowing him down. Cynthia would hear him and whisper his name, so she wouldn't knock him down.

"I'm here, I'm here, and I'm going to America." He would answer her. Cynthia smiled to herself, this was the strongest child she had ever met.

The last field they went through was by far the worst, for it had just begun to rain. Ben and Shu Lee covered grandfather's face and head with the shirt Cynthia had offered, because she was wearing a T-shirt under it. Ben encouraged everyone to start again, as he knew it would be nearly dawn when they arrived at the Embassy. Crawling out of the water with mud from head to their feet was such a relief.

They began to pick up speed, Shunlu was running again. Cynthia called his name. It was so dark and with the rain, she had no idea where he was, or what direction to follow. The path they were on was narrow and slippery from the rain.

The gunshot they heard was horrifying to all of them. They dropped to the ground and waited without saying a word, Cynthia crawled back to Ben, and told him, "I need to see about Shunlu. Shu Lee can get you there on a different path. He knows how to get to the Embassy."

Ben whispered, "Everyone must hide in the bushes that surround the Embassy. The plan is to take us in one at a time."

Cynthia crept along the path in the direction Shunlu was running before they heard the gunshot. Suddenly she heard men's voices, and they were right in front of her. She turned and stumbled down into the ditch, and found she was again standing in cold water. The men heard the splash, they began to shoot in her direction. They didn't know what, or whom they were shooting at. All she could do was crouch down as low as she could.

They walked swiftly by her. She remained in the crouching position until she could no longer hear them. Quickly, one step at a time, she got back upon the path. After she had gone nearly a quarter of a mile, she heard a noise. A little voice saying, "Help me, help me, please."

"Shunlu, Shunlu," Cynthia answered, and was so frightened at what she was going to find. She felt around on him and felt a wet spot on his shoulder. When she felt his shoulder he cried out in pain. He had been hit with the gunshot they had heard. Cynthia needed to find something to put on it for pressure to stop the bleeding. The only thing she had that was not covered with mud, was her bra, she took it off, and tied it tightly around the wound

Cynthia carefully set him up, and said, "Oh, Shunlu, I'm so sorry, I only wish it had been me. You do not deserve this."

She thought about the dirt he had all over him. He would have infection in the wound if it weren't cleaned soon. Cynthia lifted his ridged little body carefully up into her arms.

"Shunlu, Shunlu." His limp body told her he was not going to be any help at this time. He probably had lost a large amount of blood, and she knew she had to hurry. She tried to remember all the conversations about finding the American Embassy.

CHAPTER 24

When Cynthia reached the city, the sun was just beginning to come up. She was trying to run, but it was so difficult, trying not to make Shunlu's wound bleed more. She shifted his body and carried him like a mother going to the market. The streets were filling up with vendors and women wanting fresh fruit.

She had no idea what direction to go. Then she thought she heard her name, without being obvious, Cynthia kept hurrying along the street, and slowly turned her head. A man she had never seen before, dressed like a Laotian man, came up and walked by her, and as he did, he said, "Ben wants you to follow me."

She had never been a trusting person, but this was the time she needed help, she was just a few steps behind him. Blood was seeping on to her T-shirt. Shunlu could die in her arms. The first sight of the Embassy was a sanctuary of hope for her.

Her arms had held Shunlu so tightly, she could not get her arms to relax. Ben pulled one of her arms open, and then the other. She laid him on a table, for a nurse to take care of him. The nurse gave orders to fill the bath tub with water. Shunlu was caked with mud and blood.

When Shunlu's wound was cared for, he was taken to a bedroom till he regained consciousness, while the rest waited for news about their dear little friend. The nurse refused to let anyone in to see this wonderful little child till morning.

They were all having breakfast when the nurse came in to tell them Shunlu was awake. They all filed in around the bed and stood in shocked amazement. The child they knew who never had taken off his knit stocking cap, now revealed what he had hidden from them all. Beautiful, long black hair hanging to his waist.

And that was not all, the child was dressed in pink pajamas the nurse had found. The child's face was so clean for the first time, and was very pretty. The nurse stood next to the bed.

She said, "Shunlu, whom you have all thought was a boy is a brave little girl." Cynthia's eyes filled up with tears. Even Shu Lee and his grandparents did not know.

The nurse went on to say, "The streets are no place for a girl, so Shunlu did what she needed to do. Pretend to be a boy."

The first words out of Shunlu's mouth were, "I'm going to America." Everyone burst into laughter.

"The trip will have to wait," Ben told her, "Till you are well enough to travel." She smiled, and whispered to the nurse, "I'm going to America."

It took only a few days, and they all rode to the airport in a bulletproof car. Sheriff Conrad was on the plane waiting for them. When they were in their seats the feeling each one had was indescribable.

Ben, and his father, and Cynthia talked most of the flight back toward the United States. They wanted everything remembered.

The plane landed safely in Canada, as the sheriff ordered. They were all taken to the police station first. A statement had to be made by each one. Shu Lee's statement was the most important to the sheriff. He had to help his daughter free her husband's brother, because now he believed Will was innocent. Shu Lee took a lie detector test and passed it without any problems.

CHAPTER 25

The next thing the sheriff had to do was hide all of his witnesses. He put them in an army truck and during the night hours took them to a deserted army base. The base was located over the border into the United States. The truck drove up to a large quonset hut. A soldier opened the door and the driver drove in. No lights were used, only flashlights. The quonset hut was all prepared for them, it had been made into living quarters to house them all.

Cynthia was adamant about caring for Shunlu's medical needs. Shu Lee was watching over his grandparents, and Ben was in charge of everyone.

Hundraayus was now the sheriff's profound problem. Every extra man the police department had was on this case. They had men who specialized in drug trafficking, men who tracked well. They had bounty hunters looking for Hundraayus and his men. Bounty hunters were in a class of their own, because they would get paid if they caught and brought Hundraayus and his men in.

For the first time in a very long time they all slept peacefully in their army bunks, The next few days they all remained quiet and talked in low voices.

Cynthia told Ben, "I feel like a fugitive, and I'm not guilty of anything."

The man guarding the door, sat by it, day and night.

Sheriff Conrad had been busy keeping Kim hidden all the time Ben had been gone. The sheriff owned a cabin in a deserted area by a lake. The day Ben left for Laos, he had moved Kim and

Philip to his log cabin. He had the hunting commissioner take them, with a month's supply of food, so no one would suspect anyone was living in the cabin. The commissioner made rounds all over the area and watched the cabin very carefully.

The sheriff had called the cook, at the cafe, informing him, Kim had gone away to take care of her ailing grandmother, hoping Hundraayus would leave her alone.

Sheriff Conrad already had an enormous amount of information about Hundraayus, and also a huge criminal file against him. The problem was, they didn't know where he was hiding. He had simply disappeared. The sheriff's men had been watching his home, his ships, and his sewing factory.

Then the most outrageous thing happened. A bounty hunter called Sheriff Conrad, telling him, he knew where Hundraayus was, but before he would tell the sheriff, the man wanted to make sure he received the reward money.

The sheriff told him, "You have to deliver him unharmed to me, then, and only then, do you get the reward money." When the sheriff hung up the phone, the bounty hunter on the other end was still swearing.

Mike Rolin was a handsome man, with dark hair and eyes. He was well educated with a degree in law. He had just left his law office, seeking a new life with more freedom.

Mike had been stuck at a desk for nearly ten years, and one morning he awoke to the feeling of being trapped. He had grown up excelling in whatever he did.

Mike arrived at his office early on the day that would change his whole life. He thought he needed to find meaning in his life. He thought he needed some excitement, but he would find the choice he made, could have ended his life.

He explained to his elderly secretary, who knew the law as well as he did. He needed to be gone for awhile. He asked her to, "Remain, and keep the office running." He was going to do something he had thought about for along time.

Mike had learned about Hundraayus, because he had been hired to defend the six men in jail. He knew the whole story. He had studied, and investigated on his own, Hundraayus' activities.

Ben and Cynthia did not have any idea the man setting behind them on the plane to Laos was no other than Mike Rolin. His beard was now covering his handsome face, his clothing had changed from an expensive suit, to clothes of someone down on his luck. His personal identification cards were sewn into his shorts.

Mike Rolin, now bounty hunter, was calling from Laos. Hundraayus had gone there to help his men find Shu Lee. If it hadn't been for Ben and Cynthia, Shu Lee would have been killed. The bounty hunter was very careful and very shrewd. He had watched Hundraayus board one of his ships returning to America.

He immediately got a job on the ship. His job was in maintenance, cleaning, cooking and whatever he was asked to do, No one would talk to him, he tried to ask a few questions and the men would just walk away from him.

The ship was a few days out onto the ocean, and he was asked to take a cart of food to the lower part of the ship. He had no idea where he was going or why. He pushed the cart to a door where a man stood guard. The man guarding the door turned and put a key in and opened the door to push the cart in.

What the bounty hunter saw, and could also smell, was horrendously inhuman. The guard said, "Come back and get the cart, now get the hell out of here." The bounty hunter was appalled at what he had just witnessed. Without a word, he went to the latrine and was sick. It was the most intolerable situation that could happen to any human being. He couldn't get the sight out of his mind.

He knew he had to go back and get the food cart, and he knew that, as strong as he had always been, this was going to be the challenge of his life,

The memory of the men, women, and small children standing day and night, cramped together. The seasickness smell, the bathroom smell. He didn't know how many people were in the small room, but he guessed nearly forty.

It was all true, Sheriff Conrad had told all of the men on this case, what Hundraayus was promising these unsuspecting Laotians. He took all of their money and treated them barbaric. The weak would not survive.

CHAPTER 26

The bounty hunter needed to get word to Sheriff Conrad, but how? He needed to come up with an idea within the next three days, before the ship docked in the United States, and Hundraayus took all of his deprived passengers to his sewing factory.

He started back down to the bottom part of the ship. When he was at the door, the guard had the food cart out of the room, waiting to be picked up and taken to the galley. The bounty hunter tried not to look at the guard's face, he wanted to act as if he had not seen the people in the room, and that he was just doing his job. His hand reached out, and he fumbled, grabbing the handle. He hoped the guard did not notice.

He lay in his bed that night, denied of any sleep until dawn, trying to think of a way to send a message to the sheriff. It was the following day he noticed the ship was beginning to wildly jerk back and forth. He made a quick trip to the deck. The skies were filled with angry-looking clouds, and the water was churning with strong gale-like winds. The men on the deck were slipping and sliding, one yelled at him, "You man, get your dumb bun down below."

He quickly went back down to work. The thought came to him, what if the ship was really in danger. They couldn't send for help and it would serve Hundraayus right to be on board at this time.

As soon as the cook had his work done, he pushed the food cart in front of the bounty hunter, and said, "You know where to take this."

The ship was now being tossed around, and the terrifying noise of creaking, and the wind was getting stronger. He pushed the cart toward the door.

The cart was tipping from one side of the narrow passage to the other. He braced himself and the cart, because he didn't want any of the food to spill. He knew the people in the room only received one meal a day. It was a different guard at the door.

As the guard opened the door, he could hear moaning, groaning, and shrieking, and worse than that, he heard the writhing from vomiting, because of the ship's violent turbulence. The air was stifling coming out into the hall.

He told the guard he would be back for the cart. The guard just grunted at him, "You do that."

When the guard turned his back to push the food cart in, the bounty hunter got one more look into that awful hole. He saw a large pile of people, they could not stand up when the ship tipped from the huge hurricane waves. They fell on top of each other and he hoped no child was underneath. They needed help more than ever, the people on the bottom would surely die. There was no way they could eat in this storm.

He was struggling back to his bunk so he could hang onto something. He grabbed a door handle in the hallway and heard a man's voice saying, "But boss, we can't send up a flare, if we get caught, we'll all go to prison." A flare, of course, but where would he get a flare." He knew if he got caught doing something wrong, they would throw him overboard. He had one more day to find the flares, he decided he would wait until they were through the storm.

The storm continued until sunrise. When the storm was over, everything on the ship was turned upside-down, and on the floor. The rooms all had water in them, He wondered how much water was in the hole, and he wondered how many people died in that room during the storm. He was sure Hundraayus collected their money before they boarded this ship, so he probably didn't care.

The cart was back in the galley, someone else had taken it back. The bounty hunter began to help clean in the galley. When every man was busy, he slipped out of the door, and went toward the engine room. He hoped he could at least locate the flares. He wouldn't take them until he actually used them.

He hurried through the hall and down several steps. Each hall, each staircase brought him closer to the engine room. The engine room was also in disarray. The repair tools were all over the floor. The men were in a turmoil, he pretended to be picking up tools, while he looked around. The flares were hooked securely to the wall. He counted three, he would take them all. The time had to be just right.

He put his head down and worked his way to the door, and back to the galley. He heard someone yell, "Hey you, man, the boss wants his breakfast now."

The bounty hunter said, "Not me man, him." as he pointed to someone else. The cook would not stand to have a low-life worker refuse to do what he asked. The cook walked up to the bounty hunter, pushed the tray into his chest. The cook also looked very angry. The bounty hunter decided not to bicker with the cook, because he did not want to bring attention to himself.

He knocked on the door, it opened a crack, and the bounty hunter said, "Breakfast for the boss." The door opened and an arm reached out and grabbed the tray. The door slammed in his face. He really wanted to see something, but was so afraid he would drop the tray, The man was wearing a tuxedo, but he was sure it was not the boss. What he was sure of, was the boss was in the room. The room smelled clean, and the aroma was of rich cigars, unlike the room down below, that was dark, dank, and smelled of death.

After he returned to the galley, he cleaned up the cook's mess. While he worked, every minute was spent figuring out how he was going to shoot off the flares, and most of all, when. The money for capturing Hundraayus was no longer the most important factor now, it was how to save as many of the downtrodden Laotians as he could.

Mike Rolin had needed a change in his life, but he never imagined he would end up in a life and death situation. Nothing could have prepared him for this.

He knew this was the last full day on the water, that meant he needed to know when they would be docking.

The bounty hunter decided the Captain of the ship would appreciate some fresh coffee. He fixed a tray with coffee and cookies, and found his way to the bridge. The men in the wheelhouse thought nothing of his coming in. They grabbed the coffee and took a cookie, and paid no attention to him. As the last man was taking a cup from the tray, the bounty hunter asked, "When will we dock?"

The man responded absentmindedly, "At ten o'clock tonight." He left, not wanting anyone to suspect him.

The water was calm all day, and the ship was cleaned from top to bottom. The only room not cleaned was the room of death. The bounty hunter was ordered to take the food cart to the bottom. The guard standing in front of the door reached for the cart, and said, "Get out."

He left without getting a glimpse into the hellhole. He waited nearly an hour, and went back for the cart, again it was in the hall.

His afternoon and evening were spent cleaning the kitchen, and then scrubbing the deck again.

His plan had to work or he would surely die. He dressed in black, and prepared to leave for the engine room. As he approached the engine room he heard loud voices, sounding as if they were arguing. He slowly turned the door handle, and slipped inside. The six men were standing in front of an engine discussing what was wrong with it, and how they were going to keep it going for another hour till they docked.

He went to the wall where the flares were fastened. He quickly released them and took all three. He put them inside of his jacket, and left. The hiding place he had found was just inside of the life boat that was tied to the ship, next to the deck.

He had just laid the flares in the hiding place, when he heard footsteps coming toward him. He took a few steps away from the small boat, and squatted down in a dark area.

CHAPTER 27

What he saw sickened his stomach. The first two men were carrying something in a black bag. They went to the railing and threw it over. The two men following also carried a black bag. They went directly to the railing, and the bounty hunter heard another splash.

He decided he needed to shoot the flare now, if the coast guard got here they could recover the two bodies he had just seen Hundraayus' men throw overboard.

He waited until the men left, and then went to the rescue boat. He quickly got one flare out. His escape plan was to hide under a canvas in the boat. He crept across the deck of the ship to the opposite side to shoot off the flare.

The bright light lit up the dark night, and then veered to the docking shore. Immediately the ship was alive. The captain rang the warning alert and search began, every man was looking for the traitor. The men running by the bounty hunter were looking everywhere. Suddenly, a flashlight lit up the small boat, and within minutes he was found under the canvas. He was grabbed roughly, pulled out and slammed to the deck.

He was handcuffed and leg shackles were slapped on him. He felt a sharp pain, and then everything went black. Everything was so wrong, the voices, he couldn't understand what they were saying. He was trying so hard to wake up. He found he couldn't move, and was having a hard time breathing. Why were these people standing so close to him? He opened his eyes and what he saw was like a nightmare. He was in the dark, dank room. Hundraayus' men had put him there to deal with later.

The sheriff's men on shore had seen the flare, the coast guard also had seen the flare. The ship was now surrounded by flashing lights from the coast guard, and the sheriff and all of his men arrived by speed boats. The coast guard ordered the ship's captain to drop anchor, and stop all engines.

The coast guard's men boarded the ship, along with the sheriff, and all of his men, with guns ready. The sheriff ordered every man on the ship to come immediately upon the deck.

Every man was on the deck except Hundraayus and his bodyguard. The sheriff walked slowly past each man, looking for Hundraayus. When he was not found, the sheriff ordered the coast guard to take all of Hundraayus' men to the police station and jail them.

He was going to search the ship, and he did not want any of Hundraayus' men to help him escape, if he was on the ship. Hundraayus' men had sworn to him, they would protect him, even if it meant losing their own lives.

CHAPTER 28

The sheriff ordered his men to search every inch of the ship. Hundraayus and his bodyguard knew what was happening, and while everyone was up on the deck the two men slipped out of their extravagant living quarters. They headed to the horrific quarters of the Laotian's, unlocked the door, and pushed the people back so they could squeeze in. It was so dark in the room the people did not know what was happening.

The two men shoved until they were in the middle. The plan, Hundraayus told his man, "We'll go out with these low-life people. I'll pick the time and we'll escape." What Hundraayus did not know was, he and his man had pushed and shoved, and now were standing next to the bounty hunter.

When the bounty hunter was caught, Hundraayus' men put his handcuffs on while his arms were in front of him. The bounty hunter was a very clever man. Even in the dark, he was alert to everything around him.

Mike Rolin had learned early, while growing up on the streets of Los Angeles, to use all of his senses. The man standing next to him smelled of fragrant cologne, and cigars, only a rich man could smoke. He did not smell of vomit and feces. The bounty hunter slowly began to raise his handcuffed hands. When he had them high over Hundraayus' head, he swiftly put them over his head and down to his waist.

Hundraayus was taken completely by surprise and tried to move to get away, but was imprisoned by the bounty hunter's strong arms and the handcuffs.

Hundraayus yelled loudly and tried to struggle free, his bodyguard was trying to help him. The bounty hunter was yelling, "Hundraayus' man, get him away." The people were feeling the man, knowing he was not one of them. They were yanking on him, stumbling, they pulled him to the wall away from Hundraayus. In the dark, the bodyguard's clothing was torn off, and hands were all over him. He was swearing and screaming.

The sheriff and his men searched the entire ship, and this was the only door that was closed and locked. He banged on the outside of the door. The Laotian whose body was pressed up against the door, could not use his hands, so he kicked and kicked on the inside. The sheriff yelled, "Who is in there, who are you?"

The only one who could speak good English was the bounty hunter. He began yelling as loud as he could, "Get this door open now." The sheriff had no keys so his men found an ax and crowbar and started opening the door.

The door opened only enough for the first man to file out. One by one people came out, Gasping at the sight, for it was shocking and overwhelming to the sheriff and his men. Some could hardly walk, they looked sick and gaunt. The adults carried the children, who were dehydrated and weak. It was inexcusable that they had stood for nearly seven days, living in those abominable conditions.

The bounty hunter did not move until everyone was out. The bodyguard could not move, he had his coat tied over his head, and his shirtsleeves had been tied tightly around his wrists. His pants were down around his ankles. He had been moaning and crying, but no one paid any attention.

The sheriff opened the door as far as it would go. His men rushed in, Hundraayus was hollering as loud as he could, "I have not done anything wrong. I want to see my lawyer."

The bounty hunter personally turned Hundraayus over to Sheriff Conrad.

Handcuffs were fastened around his wrists. He continued to rave in a tangent. He had no regard for the meanness he had done in the lives of the Laotians, but now his life was in danger, he was experiencing panic. He continued to be difficult, twisting and turning his body. With a man on each side of him, he was taken off his ship, screaming and hollering.

The ship was impounded. Hundraayus' private room would be searched for any evidence. The sheriff had called ahead, to have the prosecuting attorney come to the police station, to see the condition of the victimized Laotians.

The police station was crowded with the Laotians being treated by a doctor. The children were crying from hunger. The immigration authorities were there. An interpreter was there. When the authorities were all finished, the Laotians were all taken to a shelter for the homeless, where they were showered and fed their first good meal in seven days. They would all remain there until homes could be found for them.

Hundraayus and his bodyguard were locked in a cell together, and could be heard in a heated argument most of the time.

The room on the ship that belonged to Hundraayus was searched. Ben and Cynthia tore it apart. They found the life savings in a large suitcase that Hundraayus had taken from the families that wanted a new life in the country of opportunity.

Shu Lee had told Ben to look in the freezer. They found the drugs Hundraayus was bringing into the states from Europe. The drugs were all packaged in plastic bags in frozen fish crates. They now had all of the evidence to send Hundraayus to prison for a very long time.

CHAPTER 29

The next few days Sheriff Conrad, Ben and Cynthia were busy getting all of the affidavits from the Laotians who would tell their story about what Hundraayus had done to them.

A little girl told the interpreter the story about her loving grandmother dying during that awful storm. She had been crushed. Her burial was merely throwing her overboard in a black bag. Now Hundraayus had murder charges brought against him.

When all of the stories had been written, anyone who heard them, felt a stabbing feeling in their heart. The people who had been in that room all knew who had been thrown overboard, that the bounty hunter had witnessed. The second bag held a young mother and her newborn baby. This was a time of grieving, it was a time of anger, the relief of being rescued, and forgiveness would come much later.

Shu Lee and his family were united in crying tears of joy. They were free to live a life they had only dreamed of. Shu Lee would be Sheriff Conrad's most important witness.

Sheriff Conrad and Mike Rolin met privately. The sheriff expressed his gratitude to him. Mike asked the sheriff to put the bounty money in an account to be used to help the people who had come under Hundraayus' unmerciful cruelty.

Sheriff Conrad sent for Kim and Philip to come home. Will and his friend had been released to the sheriff. He had decided to take full responsibility of Will, because of his carelessness. Will and his friend would live with him and his wife until the trial was over.

Cynthia had worked with Ben so closely, she couldn't think of life without him, so she asked him if he would join her in a partnership in her private detective office.

Mike Rolin walked into his office with a new outlook on life.

Shunlu was living with Cynthia, and they were planning an adoption party, Ben was the first to be invited. America was all Shunlu had dreamed it would be.

Each person who had come in contact with Hundraayus had paid a price. Each one was now free of him.

KIM'S UNPLANNED SAGA

KIM'S LIFE WAS JUST THE WAY SHE HAD DREAMED IT WOULD BE. SHE HAD HER OWN HOUSE. A NEW CAR, AND A TERRIFIC JOB.

IN ONE NIGHT HER WHOLE LIFE WAS TORN APART. AN ANGRY, HOSTILE YOUNG MAN BROKE INTO HER CAR, AND KIDNAPPED HER. HE ORDERED HER TO DRIVE UP INTO A DESOLATE MOUNTAINOUS REGION.

KIM WAS HANDCUFFED AND KEPT IN AN OLD ABANDONED CABIN, BUILT FOR HUNTERS MANY YEARS BEFORE. KIM'S ESCAPE NEARLY TOOK HER LIFE, BECAUSE THE SNOW STORM THE DAY BEFORE BROUGHT NEARLY TWO FEET OF SNOW, AND THE RAIN MADE IT NEARLY IMPOSSIBLE TO WALK.

IN DESPERATION SHE RAN FROM THE CABIN AFTER TRICKING HER CAPTOR. THE BLOWING SNOW MADE IT IMPOSSIBLE TO SEE. KIM FALLS DEEP INTO A RAVINE. THE TEMPERATURE WAS AT THE FREEZING MARK.

WHEN KIM'S CAPTOR FINDS HER, SHE IS CLOSE TO DEATH. HE SAVES HER LIFE BY TAKING HER BACK TO THE CABIN, REMOVES ALL OF HER CLOTHING, HE DISROBES, AND LAY NAKED ON TOP OF HER TO WARM HER NEARLY FROZEN BODY.

KIM AWAKENED IN THE MORNING AND FEELS EVERY PART OF HER CAPTOR'S BODY.

**COVER ART BY
JEANNIE NEMMERS**